BELIEVE

52

BELIEVE

THE VICTORIOUS STORY OF

ERIC LeGRAND

52

WITH MIKE YORKEY

HARPER

An Imprint of HarperCollinsPublishers

Harper is an imprint of HarperCollins Publishers.

Believe: The Victorious Story of Eric LeGrand
Copyright © 2012 by Eric LeGrand
Adapted for young readers by Annie Stone

Library of Congress Cataloging-in-Publication Data is available.
978-0-06-222582-5 (trade bdg.)

All photos courtesy of the author with the exception of the following (page numbers correspond to photo insert):
Page 6 (all images), page 7, page 8 (top image), page 9 (middle image and bottom image), page 16 (bottom image): Courtesy of Rutgers Athletic Communications
Page 9 (top image): Photo courtesy of the Kessler Institute
Page 11 (bottom image), page 12 (all images), page 13 (all images), page 15 (middle and bottom images): Photo by Sara Partridge
Page 16 (top image): Photo by Mike Yorkey

Book design by Joe Merkel
12 13 14 15 16 LP/RRDH 10 9 8 7 6 5 4 3 2 1

First Edition

To my mother, Karen
You've been there every step of the way
throughout this incredible journey,
and the many people who have had my back

CONTENTS

1

THE QUIET BEFORE THE DAWN

I AM CONSTANTLY COLD.

My body's been that way ever since my accident.

At one time, my body could maintain a constant temperature of about 98.6 degrees Fahrenheit, no matter how hot or cold it was outside, as long as I was wearing the right clothing, of course. My body could adjust to the heat of the sun or a chill in the air.

During the hot summer months, when I was running through a series of football drills at training camp, my body would send a signal to my brain saying, *Hey, it's getting hot around here! We need to cool things down.* And then I'd start sweating, which was good because sweat evaporates and cools down the skin.

I liked working up a good sweat on the practice field. A healthy sweat is the body's normal reaction to hot temperatures and intense physical exercise.

And when fall came around, my body reacted to cooler temperatures by making my brain tell me to put on more clothes to keep me warm.

But now, with fractured bones—called *vertebrae*—in my spinal column, the cold is unbearable. The spinal cord is home to a major collection of nerves. These nerves act as sensors that send messages about what I feel to the brain and then send the message to move from my brain to the rest of the body. All messages like this must pass through the spinal cord to reach the body's muscles, arms, and legs.

Let's say you have an itch on your nose. A message will journey from your brain, through the nerves in your spinal cord, and reach your right hand in less time than it takes to blink an eye. Once your hand receives that message to scratch your nose, your body takes the correct action to complete the task. No one likes an itchy nose. When the spinal cord is damaged, however, that message from the brain can't get through the tangle of nerves, which means you can't move your hand to satisfy that itch.

Following my accident, the column of nerves that traveled from the brain to the tailbone had gone haywire. My brain was firing messages, but the rest of my body was incapable of receiving them. The result was a sudden and complete loss of movement. I can't walk, I can't move my torso, and I can't flex my fingers or toes. And my body can no longer adjust its core temperature. My internal "thermostat" is busted.

Mom keeps the heat inside our apartment at seventy-eight degrees during the day, which is still a few degrees cooler than I'd like, but our home heating bills are high enough as it is. She usually dresses me in training outfits from my old team at Rutgers University and a sweater. If I'm still cold, she turns on a small electric heater in my bedroom. Even with the additional heat, though, I never feel completely warm.

I've told Mom that I wouldn't mind moving to Miami, although I know that's not practical at the moment. But it sure would be nice living where the temperature would be in my sweet spot—somewhere in the mid- to high eighties. I currently live in the central Jersey area of the Garden State, where the summers are warm but the winters are gray and cold.

In the spring and fall, I rarely go outside in short sleeves and can't be in the shade very long, because I need the warmth of the sun. If I go inside a commercial building, though, I don't like the air-conditioning at all, especially if a fan is blowing on me. Restaurants are the worst, especially on hot, sticky days when they crank up the AC to the maximum. During the dog days of August, it feels like I'm eating inside a refrigerator. Sometimes I shiver waiting for my food.

I travel around in a wheelchair-accessible VW Routan van with Mom behind the wheel. As soon as the ramp goes up and the side door closes, I ask Mom to turn up the heat, even on a warm fall day when the temperature reminds me of Indian summer.

I used to think those clear, sunny afternoons in October made for perfect football weather . . . not too hot, not too cold. I loved the feeling of freedom—free to run with the wind, free to make my own path, and free to knock my opponents to the ground. That's why I loved playing the game of football. My athletic body always felt warm, no matter what the temperature was outside.

Then something happened during a football game that changed my life forever.

Needing a Lift

There are a lot of things I can't do these days, simple things that I took for granted before my accident—like putting myself to bed. Mom, who's my main caregiver, has to perform that chore every night. I weigh 245 pounds—thirty pounds under my playing weight—but I'm still a big load, especially for a mother who's a hundred pounds lighter than me.

In my bedroom we have a hydraulic patient lift—also known as a Hoyer Lift—that uses a sling with straps to move me from my wheelchair to my bed. The toughest part for Mom is lifting up one of my legs at a time so that she can pull the sling through and position it under me at the same time.

When Mom is satisfied that she has me properly in the sling—and this part usually takes fifteen minutes—she brings over the Hoyer Lift, which raises me out of my chair so that she can move me over to my bed. It's kind of like one of those floor cranes you see in car repair shops to lift engines and other heavy parts.

After hooking up each strap to the top of the Hoyer

Lift, Mom can elevate or lower me as necessary. Mom rolls the Hoyer Lift toward my bed and positions it as close to the bed as she can before lowering me.

Then it's a matter of working me out of the sling, which takes some time, since the sling is mostly under my lower back and the top half of my torso. Once she's removed the sling and pushed the Hoyer Lift to the side, Mom can get me ready to sleep.

She lowers the bed to a lay-flat position and starts by taking off my pants, which must be done one leg at a time. Then she takes off my sweater, the top of my training outfit, and whatever shirt I happen to be wearing that day.

I sleep in my boxers without a shirt on, which you may think is crazy because of how cold I am all the time, but I can't wear an undershirt because I'm sleeping on a special mattress—a microAIR 95 mattress from Invacare, which automatically turns me every hour so that I won't get bedsores.

I've tried sleeping with a nightshirt, but my shirt would get twisted when the bed turned me to the right or the left. When that happened, I couldn't do anything to fix the predicament I found myself in, which meant I had to call for Mom in the middle of the night. She sleeps in the bedroom next to mine.

Mom says that I'm usually snoring within minutes of her turning out the lights and closing my bedroom door.

Every hour, my high-tech mattress moves me into a new position so that I'm not lying on the same pressure points all night long. I usually don't notice that I'm being moved around the first few hours I sleep.

My dreams are strange. In every single one of them, I'm not in my wheelchair. I'm walking around. I haven't forgotten what that feeling is like. Or sometimes I'm running on the beach, just like you see in so many commercials. I'll be tossing a football with friends, enjoying the salt air and the warm sunshine. It feels so weird because it seems so real. I really think I can catch a football again. *Wow, I can do this.*

Then my bed rotates, and my body moves, which wakes me up a bit. I try to move, and nothing happens. I realize I was just dreaming. But I don't let myself get down. I tell myself, *Maybe it's not today. Maybe it's another day.* I know one day it will shockingly happen. Maybe I'll be able to lift a finger, or maybe I'll be able to lift one of my arms. When that happens, everyone will be shocked. I'm waiting for that day to come. I know God has a plan for something like that.

I fall back asleep, and the dreams start all over again. I'll be walking again, or lifting up a spoonful of ice cream to eat, but around four or five o'clock in the morning, I stir from being automatically turned around again. There's not much else I can do except to lie half-awake in the darkness, surrounded by my thoughts. It's at those times when my mind takes me to places that I don't want to revisit—like that horrible afternoon at New Meadowlands Stadium.

The date is etched in my memory: October 16, 2010.

We were playing Army at the Meadowlands, and we were down a touchdown, 17-10, with ten minutes to go in the fourth quarter. The Black Knights were on our forty-six-yard line, but they faced a third-and-eight to keep their drive going.

"Time for a stop!" yelled my buddy, linebacker Antonio Lowery, as we broke from our huddle. Army already had three first downs on this drive, and they were marching down the field. We had to hold them to keep it a one-score game.

I was a nose guard, the player who lines up off the center. At 275 pounds, I usually gave up a good twenty-five to thirty pounds to the beefy dudes on the front line.

But our head coach, Greg Schiano, liked his defensive linemen to be a tad smaller and a lot quicker, and that's where I fit in.

I took my three-point stance and remembered from our film sessions that Army had this play where they pulled the guard and the fullback would try to take you out, opening a big hole for their running back, Jared Hassin, who, at six feet, three inches and 235 pounds, liked to square up his shoulders and run north-south. Hassin was tough to bring down when he had a head of steam behind him; he had already run on us for a hundred yards.

Both teams lined up for this big third-down play, and I waited for the snap of the ball. Their quarterback, Trent Steelman, was going through his cadence as players moved around before the hike of the ball. I sensed something, so I shifted over a yard or two to place myself in the gap between the guard and the center hiking the ball. Sure enough, on the snap, the guard went out, but instead of following him, I maintained my ground for a split second and then shot through the gap, slipping past the other guard who was assigned to block me.

Suddenly I was in the Army backfield, and their quarterback handed the ball off to Hassin. I popped him pretty good in the chest and nailed him to the ground for a one-yard loss. It was a good hit.

I pulled myself up to celebrate, but my head was buzzing. I saw some stars. My teammate Scott Vallone, a six-foot-three-inch defensive tackle, was going crazy with joy, giving me a chest bump as my other teammates came over to congratulate me. But I had been dinged. I guess I hit Hassin with my head, because something was definitely not right.

Feeling woozier by the second, I went on autopilot. It was fourth down. I knew I had to get off the field. I started trudging toward the sideline—and looked up to see nothing but white uniforms and gold helmets.

What's going on? Then it hit me. I was going the wrong way. I was making my way toward the Army sideline.

There was a lot of confusion because the Black Knights were sending out their punt team, and we were putting our punt/block team onto the field, so it was pretty crowded out there.

"Hey, Eric!" Scott yelled amid the confusion.

This wasn't my sideline. I had to go the other way. Knowing that I was running out of time, I began sprinting back to our bench before Army snapped the ball.

No one on our sideline noticed that I had been going the wrong way. Several happy coaches came over and tapped me on the helmet. "Good job!" each of them yelled, fired up because we had made a crucial fourth-quarter stop in a close game.

I found a place on the bench and took off my helmet. Maybe I had a slight concussion out there on the field. No, that wasn't it. I had had a concussion playing football one time—back in Jr. Pee Wees during my Pop Warner days—and this wasn't a concussion. But I definitely felt something, like the gong of a bell.

I drank some water and took a few minutes to catch my breath. Then our fans started cheering like crazy. An Army punt had us pinned back at the seven-yard line, but D. C. Jefferson caught a long ball for a fifty-three-yard gain. Eight plays later, QB Chas Dodd hit Mark Harrison with a sixteen-yard touchdown pass, and we were back in the game: 17-17.

"Kickoff team!" yelled our special teams coach, Robb Smith.

That was my cue. Besides playing defense for half the snaps, I was a special-teamer, a member of the "bomb squad" on kickoff coverage. My job was to sprint down the field while the ball was in the air and annihilate any blockers, fill any running lanes, and knock the kick returner to the ground. Those who were part of the kick-off coverage team played with a lot of spirit and reckless abandon. You had to play that way, because a tackle deep in your opponent's territory—like inside the twenty-yard line—often set the tone for the next series of plays.

I took my position next to our kicker, San San Te, who had a good leg. I was to his immediate left.

We were set. The head referee blew his whistle and circled his right arm, and our fans rose to their feet. My heart rate always notched up several levels for kickoff.

San San took several mincing steps, and I let him pass. He was about to plant his left foot when a gust of wind blew the ball off the tee.

Time to reload.

San San reset the ball on the tee, and on the next whistle by the referee, his kick lofted into the autumn air.

Little did I know that everything about my life was about to change.

2

WHERE MY STORY STARTS

LIFE CAN CHANGE IN the flash of an eye.

I didn't know that concept very well growing up, but Mom sure did.

I was a three-year-old preschooler when my uncle, James Edward LeGrand Jr., and his girlfriend had gone into Manhattan for a jazz concert on a Saturday night. They were driving home at two a.m. on the New Jersey Turnpike when they came up on Exit 12—their exit.

Uncle Jimmy was at the wheel of his Isuzu Trooper when a drunk driver plowed into the back of his car.

Unfortunately, my uncle wasn't wearing his seat belt, and the collision killed him. His girlfriend survived, but it took her nearly a year of physical therapy before she healed. She wasn't wearing her seat belt either.

Mom said her brother's tragic death hit the family hard. He was only thirty-two years old with a lot of life to live. My grandmother, Betty Jean, continually asked herself, *Why him?* His death was quite a shock to my family, who had lost my grandfather, James Edward LeGrand Sr., only three and a half years earlier. He had died of lung cancer at the age of fifty, just four months before I was born.

The death of her father and the sudden, tragic loss of her brother was a vivid reminder to Mom that life can change just like that—in the blink of an eye.

It was through these tragedies that Mom persevered. She taught me that life goes on and that a positive outlook is important. Mom and I are very close. She has always been my number one fan on the sidelines and away from the playing field.

My Beginnings

My mom has always been a very strong and independent person. She raised her first daughter, my older sister, Nicole, as a single parent while working to support herself and Nicole. Nicole was around five years old when Mom starting dating my father, Donald McCloud, and eventually became pregnant with me. I was born on September 4, 1990, at Elizabeth General Hospital.

My parents didn't get married, but they lived together for the first five years of my life. Mom was cast in the role as the mother and the father in the relationship, and she wanted Nicole and me to grow up with her values and her morals. She wanted us to believe in God and learn the Golden Rule—treating others as we would want to be treated.

I remember one time in first or second grade, I came home with a clenched fist. "What's in your hand?" Mom asked.

I opened my hand and showed her a half dozen plastic tire valve caps.

"Where did you get those?"

"Ah, I took them off cars."

"What's wrong with you, boy?" She turned me right around and opened the front door. "Eric, you go back and you put those caps back on every single car that you took them off of."

That wasn't going to fly in Mom's house. She also wanted me to learn the same strong work ethic that she had been taught by her father and mother. My grandparents—and therefore my mother—believed that nothing was given to you, not in this life.

Mom was also determined that her children would not make some of the same mistakes she had made. She hadn't finished college before having Nicole, so she always told me in no uncertain terms: "You go to high school, you go to college, you finish college, and then you get a good job. You live the right way."

I was heading into first grade when my father moved out, the same year Mom purchased—with my grandmother's help—our first home in Avenel. Avenel is a real melting pot with a strong sense of community—about half the population is white, 20 percent is African-American, 20 percent is Asian, and 10 percent is Hispanic. Mom felt Avenel would be a great place to raise an energetic young boy.

I was certainly energetic in those early years. I wanted what I wanted from early on and was determined to get it. I was frequently raising Mom's blood pressure as a kid, but she likes to tell me one story in particular. When we were living in an apartment in nearby Woodbridge, the top floor had a finished attic, where I slept in a crib next to Mom's bed. Nicole slept downstairs in the other bedroom.

I was a toddler, two or three years old, when one day I decided I was going to ride my toy horse down the steep wooden stairs. Mom tried to stop me, but in a flash I pointed my toy pony down the stairs and pushed off. I'm told that I lasted for about three steps before tumbling down the stairs and landing in a heap.

Mom chased after me, scared to death about what shape I'd be in on the landing, but I was fine. I didn't cry. I just wanted to find out what my limits were.

It seems that I tested my limits pretty regularly when I was young, like the time I collected fireflies in a glass jar back in elementary school. Mom put holes in the top of the aluminum lid so the fireflies could breathe and gave me explicit instructions not to bring the fireflies into the house. "Leave them outside in the backyard," Mom sternly warned.

Well, I decided that my menagerie of fireflies wasn't getting enough air on a particularly warm summer evening, so I brought them inside and made the air holes bigger. I was in my bedroom, lying on my bed, and the next thing I knew, I heard Mom screaming from her bedroom, where she was watching TV. I ran in to see what the commotion was about, and she said, "Look at all the fireflies!"

Sure enough, those creatures were flying around Mom's bedroom, shining their lights and circling her bed. Mom got after me pretty good that night.

Mom wasn't the only person whose patience I tried. I didn't like to listen to my older sister, even though she was a *lot* older than me. When I was four and Nicole was fifteen and in high school, she babysat me and had the difficult task of putting me to bed. I gave her my typical hard time—I didn't want to go to bed and was in no mood to obey my older sister.

"You will do what I say!" Nicole retorted.

"No, I won't!" I fired back.

We got into a tussle when she tried to pick me up and physically *make* me go to bed. I fought back, even though I was so much younger than Nicole was. I was such a strong little kid that Nicole couldn't take me. The only way she got control over me that night was by sitting on me. That's where she put her weight advantage to good use.

Nicole will tell you that I was a brat. If she told me that I had to eat dinner before Mom came home to take me to Pop Warner football practice, I told her I didn't want to eat dinner. Then she'd repeat her order, and I'd cross my arms and shake my head. I used to think I was the "man of the house" when Mom left, and that meant I had to be a little tough guy.

Testing Mom

During the first few years of elementary school, I went to the Little Fiddler day-care center after school because Mom had to work, and I knew I had no choice. Little Fiddler was next door to my elementary school, so one of the teachers would pick me up when class was over.

In fourth grade, though, I decided I was too big for Little Fiddler.

"Ma, I don't want to go to day care any longer," I announced one day as we ate dinner. "I'm bigger than everyone else at Little Fiddler. I want to just come home after school."

Mom thought for a minute. Even though I was the youngest in my fourth-grade class, I was still the biggest kid. "All right. We'll try this," she said, and Mom made a plan. Each morning, she gave me a key to the house with instructions that I was to take the school bus home and then call her at work as soon as I stepped inside the front door. And then I would have to stay inside until she got home.

By this time, my older sister, Nicole, had gone to

college, so she wasn't around to look after me while Mom was still at work.

I was good about following Mom's directions to stay in the house after school, but I still tested my limits, frequently calling Mom at work.

"Can Dougie come over? We're just going to watch some TV."

"No, Eric. I don't want anyone coming into the house."

Then I would make five more phone calls to her, each one just like the previous one. I wouldn't give up until she said, "Okay, Eric, fine. Dougie can come over, but no one else."

But overall I was a good kid. I wasn't a problem for anybody. I didn't take advantage of the freedom Mom gave me, because I knew not to go out until she came home from work. But when she did get home, I was all over the neighborhood.

I'd usually be three or four blocks away playing basketball in someone's driveway or playing football in the park. But Mom didn't like being uninformed about where I was.

"I understand you're playing, but I need to know where you are," she said one day.

"Yes, Mom."

I tried to be better, but then I would get so caught up playing basketball with my friends that I wouldn't even come home for dinner.

Finally, Mom got me one of those prepaid phones. "This phone is for me," she said. "When I call you, you come home."

The problem was that Mom was always breaking up a good basketball or football game. I hate to admit it, but I had an iron will to do what I wanted to do. I was a social kid and wanted to be with my friends and play outside from sunup to sundown, so if Mom didn't let me go out and play, I'd moan and complain to get my way. Thankfully, I eventually grew out of those traits, but it took some time.

Even when I had friends over, I still tested Mom's patience. When I was seven or eight years old, three friends and I were messing around in a small plastic pool in our backyard. Nana was there, too.

"Get out—it's time to eat the hot dogs and hamburgers," Mom called from the barbecue, where she was tending to the meat on the grill.

My friends obeyed, but I was fine where I was. "No, I'm not getting out," I said. I probably wasn't hungry.

"What?" my mom exclaimed. "Get out of the pool now!"

She closed the distance between the barbecue and the pool, leaned in close to me, and *whoosh*, I splashed her with the biggest water splash that I could.

Mom, her face dripping wet, flared with anger. I immediately jumped out of the pool and ran to the house for protection.

"Don't you run into that house wet!" she yelled.

Forget this. I'm not getting a whuppin'. I sprinted through the house, dripping wet, and made it safely to my bedroom.

Or so I thought. Mom chased after me and cornered me in front of my bedroom door.

I snuck through her legs somehow and started running for the back door, and just before I could return to the backyard, I felt this *thwack* against my back from a ruler. The blow broke the wooden ruler in two.

I screamed, then moaned, "Ohhh, my back."

But I wasn't going to give her the satisfaction of seeing me cry. I ran and jumped back into the pool to get rid of the stinging.

Meanwhile, my friends had their mouths open from what they had just witnessed, and my grandma seemed amused by the events, but that was the last time Mom would ever smack me.

She hadn't spanked me that much before, and that incident proved that corporal punishment wasn't going to do the discipline job anymore. She had to find a new way to make me obey, so that's what Mom did. She started grounding me. I can tell you that I took Mom very seriously after that. All I wanted was to be outside playing with my friends, so when she took away that privilege, I had to shape up.

That wasn't the easiest thing to do back in elementary school. Fortunately, Mom got me involved in sports when I was in kindergarten, and I was able to learn lessons about life on and off the field from a very young age.

The Youngest and the Biggest

Birthdays were always a big deal for me. Maybe it was because September 4 always fell around Labor Day and was the last big summer holiday before school started. We usually did something fun, like inviting some friends to join us at Chuck E. Cheese's, McDonald's, or the skating rink. When I was seven or eight, I wanted to invite a very special guest—Batman. I guess I had seen the *Batman &*

Robin movie that came out that year.

So where do you find Batman? That's what Mom wanted to know. She checked out the Yellow Pages and hired Batman to show up at my party, a barbecue in our backyard. We had gorgeous weather that day, and I was in my glory. I loved having my picture taken with Batman.

Because of my September birthday, I was four years old when I entered kindergarten, which made me the youngest in my class. I suppose Mom could have held me back, but I was already bigger than all the other kids, even though many of them were six, nine, or even ten months older than me. This set a pattern that would follow me right into college.

I can still remember how, right after moving to Avenel, I would stand on a jungle gym in our backyard and look over the fence to see the other boys in the neighborhood play. Every weekend, I used to stand there for hours watching them go up and down the street, riding their bikes or throwing a ball around.

"Why don't you go out there and ask them to play with you?" Mom asked a few weeks after we moved in.

I was all embarrassed, but Mom finally convinced me to knock on one of their doors.

I knew where this one kid lived, so I gathered my

courage and walked to the house down the street. A mother answered my knock. "Do you have any kids I can play with?" I asked.

"Sure, young man," and that's how I came to know Joey Brannigan, Doug Tobias, and Charlie Schwartz. Joey and Dougie were my age, but Charlie was five years older than us, so he was our leader. They were all white, but you know, back then color didn't mean anything. We just got together and had fun playing in my sandbox, riding our bikes, and building ramps for jumps. My daredevil days had not ended with riding a toy horse down a wooden stairwell.

If it was Dougie, Joey, and me, then we would play with our Matchbox cars or play tag or Manhunt. But when Charlie came around, we usually played a game called Kill the Man with the Ball. You can figure out the point of that game.

Whatever we were doing, Charlie showed no mercy on us. When we were older and started playing basketball in one of the driveways and someone went in for a layup, Charlie would send him flying into the basketball pole or garage door. That hurt!

Charlie told us to be tough. "Don't cry," he'd say. "Get back up."

Since Charlie was the oldest, we always tried to impress him, so we dusted ourselves off and got back into the game. You couldn't complain. That was an unwritten rule in my neighborhood.

Just before I started kindergarten, Mr. Tobias told Mom that he was going to sign up Doug for Pop Warner football and thought I should play too because of my size and energy. Mom thought putting me into Pop Warner football was a great idea. Since I had tons of energy, why not get it out running up and down a football field?

I started playing in the Pop Warner flag division just before I turned five in September. Once again I was one of the youngest players in a division for five-, six-, and seven-year-olds, which had a weight limit of seventy-five pounds.

In Pop Warner flag football, no tackling was allowed. You ran until another player grabbed one of the flags on a belt around your waist. The coaches were going to put me on the line because of my size, but when they saw me run, they had second thoughts. They moved me to running back because I was so fast.

Football was pretty simple when all us kids were little shrimps. The head coach usually told me to take the handoff from the quarterback and run around the corner. That's what I always did, and most kids weren't fast enough to catch me.

Mom liked watching Pop Warner and never missed a play. She also put me into Little League baseball, and when I got a little older, I started playing youth basketball, too. I liked all three sports, and when I was younger, I didn't have a favorite.

After two seasons of flag football, just as I was about to turn seven, I finally got to play *real* football in the Mitey Mites division of Pop Warner. Helmets and pads. Tackling to the ground. Football became a lot more serious, even if we were only seven or eight years old. At least, that's how the coaches made us feel. They had us practice a lot . . . several times a week. And then we had our games every Saturday.

I didn't understand why I had to practice so much. I'd rather just play in the games than practice. But Mom told me that once you commit to something, you commit to it 100 percent. You can't just show up on game day and expect to play.

I told Mom that practice was boring, but she told me that didn't matter. I still had to go. "Get your uniform on," she'd say. When I would still give her a hard time, she would remind me about the commitment I'd made to the team. "You do not miss practices. You will not do that."

I got the message, and it contributed to the development of a strong work ethic, which has helped tremendously with my rehabilitation efforts. I grew up knowing that you practice every single day. You give it your all in training, and then you play the game. That's the reward, stepping onto the field with referees who blow the whistle to start the game.

In the Mitey Mites, the coaches placed me at running back and safety. Mom didn't understand why I was playing safety, because when she looked at the safety position in the colleges and pros, he was the guy covering the receivers when they go long. I told her that the safety in Pop Warner was more like playing linebacker. I did make a lot of tackles in Pop Warner, so what I said made sense.

When I played on the offensive side of the ball, I was a tough runner to bring down. I'd usually drag three kids along behind me, even though they grabbed my legs and ankles and hung on for dear life. I was too big for them. I would just keep my legs moving as I dragged would-be tacklers down the field.

My mom truly was my number one fan. Every time I took off on a long running play toward the end zone, my mother would run down the sideline alongside me, yelling, "Go! Go!" She was crazy out there, running and cheering me on while I was sprinting for the end zone. The other parents got a laugh out of it and would tease her every time she chased after me, but Mom says she let the excitement get the best of her. Mom was definitely the parent who, when she went to the game, she watched the game. She understood what was going on. She was very much into football.

I never witnessed Mom running behind me while I was making a long run because I was too busy looking to see if any defenders were going to catch me. It's a good thing too, because I probably would have stopped in the middle of my run, put my hands on my hips, and said to her, "Are you kidding me?"

3

A WEIGHTY PROBLEM AND A HEFTY ATTITUDE

EVEN THOUGH I WAS a handful growing up, Mom learned how to use that to her advantage at times.

It was in fifth grade that I began my obsession with sneakers. I was flipping through the pages of an Eastbay sports catalog and my eyes landed on the most beautiful pair in the world: the Nike Air Hyperflights.

I'm talking about jaw-dropping, flashy kicks that looked like they dropped down from Mars. NBA stars Jason Williams, Damon Stoudamire, and Derek Fisher were wearing them, and they were so cool. The shoes came in assorted colors, including a shiny, eye-popping cherry-red upper shell and black trim. These sneakers practically screamed, *Hey, look at me!*

I wanted to be the coolest kid in the neighborhood, the envy of Joey, Dougie, and Charlie. And those shoes would make me just that. But when I looked at the price in the catalog, my heart sank. Eastbay wanted $130 for a pair of Hyperflights.

I showed Mom the Eastbay catalog and pointed to the red sneakers. "Mom, can you get me a pair? I'll take care of them. I promise."

Mom rolled her eyes and gave me one of those *Are you kidding me?* looks. "I'm not buying a hundred-and-thirty-dollar pair of shoes just so you can go and dog them up in a week or two," she said.

"No, Mom, I won't mess them up. I'll be real careful when I go outside. I promise."

Mom hesitated, which I knew was a good sign. She was thinking about it.

"Please, Mom. They're great shoes."

"Well, if you want a pair that badly, you're going to have to earn them."

"What do you mean I have to earn them?"

"Tell you what. If you bring home good grades on

your next two tests, then we'll see."

I took that as a yes. From then on, I made sure I paid attention in class and studied extra hard. I did bring home an A and a B on my next two tests. I usually didn't get too many As, so I figured I was in the clear.

Mom studied my test results, then met my eyes. "Let me think about it," she said.

That wasn't good enough. "What do you mean, you'll think about it? You told me if I bring home good grades on my tests, I could get the shoes, and I did that."

It wasn't easy earning those good grades. I had attention problems, and instead of listening to the teacher, I was often the kid talking and messing around in class. Once the sneakers were on the line, though, I shaped up. Mom hesitated again. "I need two more weeks of good grades," she said.

Well, those two weeks turned into a whole semester. When my report card arrived in the mail, I had all As and one B. Mom saw that her little "reward" system worked, so true to her word, she got me my pair of Nike Air Hyperflights. The red beauties could be spotted a block away.

I wore my Hyperflights to class every day. Some of the kids teased me because they were so red, but I didn't care what anyone said. I knew I had worked hard to get those shoes. I loved the feeling I got after putting so much effort into something and then seeing it happen.

I didn't wear my red sneakers on the football field, of course, where Mom made sure I wore good cleats. After playing two years of Mitey Mites, the next division up was called Jr. Pee Wee, which was for eight-, nine-, and ten-year-olds who didn't weigh more than 105 pounds. At the age of eight, I was *barely* under the weight limit for Jr. Pee Wees, but by the time I was about to turn nine, I had blown past 105 pounds and had to move up to the Pee Wee division, where players weighed between 75 and 120 pounds. In Pee Wees, players could be a year older—eleven years of age.

This would set a pattern throughout Pop Warner football, where I would always be playing against kids who were one or two years older than me because I was too big for my peers. I didn't mind being one of the youngest players on the field, though. I figured that playing against older, heavier opponents would just make me a better player in the long run.

Touchdown Treats

Even while playing against older, bigger kids, I still gave Mom plenty of reasons to chase me down the sideline. I ran for a lot of touchdowns, and every kid loves to cross the goal line carrying the ball and celebrate with his teammates. I was no different.

Mom rewarded me for scoring touchdowns by baking me chocolate chip cookies. I had a special way of eating Mom's chocolate chip treats: I'd set a paper napkin on the kitchen counter next to a glass of milk, and I'd place one warm cookie on each corner and a fifth cookie in the center.

Hitting home runs got the homemade chocolate chip dessert treatment as well. I played a lot of baseball games in elementary and middle school and loved the sport as much as football. Sometimes we had either practice or a game every day from March to June.

In Little League baseball, I was always one of the *oldest* kids on the team. And there was no weight limit, so I was also one of the biggest kids out there. I was a pitcher and a center fielder, but pitching was what I liked best. I was really competitive. I wanted to strike everyone out. I took it as an insult if someone got a hit off me. When I was pitching, I didn't want to let my team down, so I rocked and fired. I just did not want to lose.

During one game, I was brought in at the bottom of the sixth and last inning with the bases loaded and no outs. I had to protect a one-run lead. It was time to shine.

I straddled the rubber and got into the zone by humming a 50 Cent song I'd heard on the radio that morning. I knew I had to strike out the side with the bases loaded. There were no other options. So that's exactly what I did. Even though the pressure was on, I went about my business.

I was a good pitcher who struck out a lot of people in Little League. I could pitch over seventy miles an hour according to the radar gun, which is pretty fast when the pitcher's rubber is only forty-six feet from the plate. My catcher would wear a dirt bike glove inside his catcher's mitt because my fastball stung his hand so bad.

My dream, like every other kid who played baseball, was to make it to Williamsport, Pennsylvania, site of the Little League World Series. Our Woodbridge Township All-Star team made a good run at getting there. We won the district and section levels, and then in the state championship we needed to beat Toms River—a New Jersey team that had won the Little League World Series in Williamsport five years earlier when they beat Kashima, Japan, in the final game, televised on ESPN. If we defeated Toms River for the 2003 state championship, then we'd go on to the regional tournament and be just one step from Williamsport.

I pitched the game to get us into the final round with Toms River. But after that I was out of innings. (Little League pitchers are allowed to pitch only six innings a week in order to save their arms.) I couldn't pitch against Toms River, and we needed to win to keep our hopes for Williamsport alive. The game was tied in the bottom of the sixth inning with Toms River at bat. They had a runner on third with two outs when their batter hit a lazy fly ball to our right fielder. If he caught the ball, we would go into extra innings.

I watched in horror as the pop fly bounced off our right fielder's glove, and the winning run scored easily. Our Williamsport dreams were over.

I ran off the field from my center-field position and threw my glove against the back of the dugout wall. Then I sat down and bawled my eyes out. I thought the world had come to an end.

This was the first and only time I ever cried after a game, and that's because going to Williamsport meant so much to me. Eventually, the sun did come up the next morning, and I recovered. Even though we were no longer in the running for the state championship, there was still a consolation game to play. I was eligible to pitch in that game, which we won. But the disappointment from losing the day before took a while to get over.

Growth Spurt

Throughout the middle school years, I played in youth basketball leagues in winter, Little League baseball in the spring and summer, and Pop Warner in the fall, but I ran into a problem as I was entering eighth grade, which would be my last year of Pop Warner football.

I weighed too much. That summer before the season started, I weighed 165 pounds. I had also gone through a growth spurt and stood five feet, eleven inches, with the squeakiest voice ever. I had grown so fast that my shoe size went from size eight to size twelve in a year, skipping right past several shoe sizes. Those red Nike Hyperflights in my closet looked like little kid shoes all of a sudden.

My weight presented a problem for Pop Warner football, since the weight limit for the Midget division was 145 pounds. That limit was raised to 170 pounds in 2012, but back in 2003, I'd have had to lose twenty pounds if I wanted to play another season.

My Pop Warner coach was Jack Nevins, who was like a father figure to me. When I told him about my weight problem, he said, "You know, you don't have to do this.

You can start lifting and get ready for high school football next year."

I couldn't imagine going a whole season without playing football. "No, Coach, this is something I really wanna do. I want to play. This is what I love to do."

"All right," he said. "But it's not going to be easy losing that much weight, especially for a growing boy like you."

I was super motivated, though. I talked to Mom about going on some type of diet and ramping up my exercise program. We decided that I'd go on a Slim-Fast diet, where I'd have a Slim-Fast shake for breakfast and lunch, and then I'd eat a healthy dinner without snacking during the day or having dessert after dinner. For exercise, I decided to run four miles a day on a treadmill that we had in the basement. Two miles in the morning, two at night.

You should have seen me working over that poor treadmill. I nearly wore off the moving belt. It was so hot in August, the basement turned into a sauna. Then I really ramped things up by putting on a T-shirt, two sweatshirts, two pairs of sweatpants, two pairs of socks, *and* a black plastic garbage bag underneath my sweatpants. With a garbage bag and so many layers of clothes on my body, I heated up on the treadmill like a Thanksgiving turkey being cooked in a plastic bag. The sweat poured off in buckets.

Sometimes I'd run outside after dinner—still wearing a garbage bag under two pairs of sweatpants—with my friends Doug Tobias, Jerry Venterelli, and Ralph Eastman. They joined me because they also had to lose a few pounds to make weight, so we tried to have some fun with it.

Losing twenty pounds in eighth grade just so I could play football wasn't easy, but I did drop all that weight and became eligible to play Midgets. But I had to keep that weight off the entire season, because we had weigh-ins every week.

Losing that weight gave me a great deal of confidence and determination. I proved to myself that I could indeed give up Mom's homemade chocolate chip cookies and brownies to keep my weight under 145 pounds. Well, not completely. I might have treated myself to a brownie after a big win, but that's all I was going to get.

Sometimes the pressure to keep my weight under the limit showed up in my attitude on the football field. One time at practice, I got into a pushing match with Nate Brown. Coach Jack had to separate us, but Nate and I had a history that dated back to fifth-grade recess. We were playing kickball in the school yard, and our team was down two runs with the recess bell about to ring. The bases were loaded, and I was up. If I gave the ball a good kick, we'd tie the game and maybe even win it.

But Nate wouldn't roll the ball up to the plate. In fact, he held on to the ball and refused to pitch to me.

"Pitch the ball!" I screamed.

"No!" he yelled back, cradling the reddish rubber ball in his arm.

"You punk! Let me kick it!"

Nate held the ball for nearly five minutes as players from both sides screamed at him. Then the recess bell went off, and we ended up losing the game.

Nate and I were both supercompetitive. During this one particular fight at practice, we gave each other some good shoves. I was ready to throw a punch, but something inside told me to drop my arms and let it go. When Nate saw me back off, he relaxed as well. I flashed a smile, and he returned a smile. Believe it or not, that was the start of a beautiful friendship.

Today, Nate is one of those people who has stood by me during some of my darkest moments. I'm glad our friendship hasn't changed one little bit over the years.

A Valuable Lesson

While I saw Coach Jack as a father figure, the other coaches—Coach Cheesy and Coach Seaford (I have no idea what their real names or last names were)—were high school students, so I figured they wanted to make the lives of little eighth graders miserable.

They would make us run laps for what seemed like no reason or do bear crawls for what seemed like the slightest mess-up or tiny infraction. If they didn't like our attitude, they'd stop practice and order us to do wind sprints.

One time, Coach Jack wasn't at practice, so Coach Cheesy and Coach Seaford were in charge. We were winning nearly all our games and having a great season, so I thought we could afford to slack off a bit. In fact, that was the general attitude among my teammates.

Not Coach Cheesy and Coach Seaford. They sensed the lack of effort, so they made everyone on the team—including Nate, Ralph, Doug, and me—run extra laps at the end of practice. I whispered to my teammates, *I'm gonna come in last.* A lot of guys followed my slow pace.

After taking our sweet time around the football field, Coach Cheesy and Coach Seaford announced that practice wasn't over.

"Line up on the sideline for wind sprints," Coach Cheesy announced. We did one after another until our tongues were hanging out of our mouths. They yelled at us to keep our feet moving. They really pushed us.

News of our lackadaisical effort reached the ears of Coach Jack. At our next practice, he took me aside and delivered a tough-love message.

"Eric, I've noticed in our games that you're not blocking out there, so we're not going to give you the ball until you start blocking," he declared. "I've seen you going through the motions. You're whiffing at guys. I can tell."

Until he said that, my attitude out there was the same as being a pitcher: *Coach, just give me the ball. Just give me the ball.* Didn't the results speak for themselves? I gained a lot of yards every game and scored a lot of touchdowns. We were winning nearly all our games. Wasn't that the point of playing?

But Coach Jack saw the bigger picture. I wasn't a team player and hadn't been for a few seasons. I wasn't blocking like I should, which meant I was letting my team down on plays when I *didn't* get the ball.

I nodded to Coach Jack that I understood.

"Here's what we're going to do, young man," he said.

"We're going to go back to basics and teach you how to block."

And that's what we did. I got a private tutorial in blocking, and we started from scratch. I had to learn to block all over again—and then block in our games and protect the quarterback from the pass rush. A funny thing happened: Even though I was following orders and blocking, it was still a couple of weeks before I started getting the ball again. But that only made me hungrier to play well.

I learned an invaluable lesson during my last season of Pop Warner: *Listen to your coaches.* They are there to make you a better player individually and make you a better player for the team. From then on out, I determined that I would do what my coaches told me to do, no matter what level of football I played.

Back in eighth grade, I didn't believe Coach Jack when he told me that if I didn't block, I wouldn't get the ball. I thought he wanted to win as badly as I did, and we both knew that our team had a better chance of victory when I ran the ball a lot. I thought Coach Jack would give me the ball because he liked me.

It turned out that Coach Jack disciplined me precisely *because* he did like me. Otherwise, he could have let me become a lazy blocker, someone who put myself before the team. If he had gone in that direction, I would have become an average player, all because of my lack of effort.

Thanks to him, I changed things around quickly. Boom! I started shoving bodies all over the place on the practice field, and those after-practice sprints—where before I didn't care if I came in last—turned into all-out bursts of pure speed from sideline to sideline. Sure, my lungs were about to explode and my legs felt like jelly, but I had to leave it all on the field.

Setting Sights High

I'm glad that Coach Jack, Coach Cheesy, and Coach Seaford didn't let me take the easy way out, and I owe them a lot. They were role models at a time when I needed one.

The situation with my father was, well, complicated. We had a good relationship when he lived with Mom and me, but it was like this in our home: What my mom said was what went. My father was never much of a disciplinarian anyway.

I used to sleep downstairs with him when we moved into the new house in Avenel back when I was in kindergarten. But I was so young the day he came and told me that he was moving out and wouldn't be living with me any longer. He said he was moving to Carteret, about three or four miles away. "Okay, Dad" was all I could say.

I didn't really understand what was going on. I was too young. But I had to adjust to one parent, and that wasn't easy.

There was still some contact with my father after he left. He would take me fishing every now and then, but I never saw him at any of my football, basketball, or baseball games when I started elementary school. I just thought that was the way things were. When I was in middle school, though, he called my mother and asked her if she thought I would mind if he came to some of my games.

"Why don't you ask him?" Mom said.

So Dad called me up and said, "Would you mind if I came to watch you play?"

"No," I replied. "But you never came before. I thought you didn't care."

"I always cared about you, Son, but I didn't think you'd want me showing up at your games."

"Yeah, you can come," I said. After that, I saw my

father at nearly all my games—football, basketball, and baseball.

During my final season of Pop Warner football, Mom gave me a set of weights for my birthday. They gathered dust throughout the fall, but after my attitude adjustment, I knew that I would have to work hard with those weights if I wanted to be an impact player in high school. I didn't know anything about how to go about that, however, so I asked my aunt's boyfriend, Ariel, if he would come up with a workout plan for me that I could start after my last Pop Warner game. Uncle Ariel—he's since married Auntie Cheryl—came up with an intense daily plan that would increase my muscle strength and give me some pop on the football field.

I made a commitment to myself that every single day I was going to work out to make myself a stronger and better football player. Then I asked my friend Nate Brown if he'd join me. Sure, he said, but he lasted only two weeks.

That was okay. Nothing was going to stop me. I went from being barely able to lift anything to benching 185 pounds going into Colonia High School for my freshman year.

By the time I started my freshman year, I had a favorite sport—football. Sure, I played baseball and basketball and liked those sports too, but football gave me the biggest adrenaline high. Nailing a runner to the ground or running for a touchdown was awesome. No other sport could compare to football.

I loved how all the hard work of practice during the previous week and year was poured into those two or three hours on the field. It was a rush to play the game; when I would make a play—the long run or the open-field tackle—there was nothing better than that.

When it came to playing football, I was all in from the top of my helmet to the cleats on my shoes.

4

THE UNEXPECTED CALL-UP

JUST BEFORE THE START of the school year at Colonia High, there was a major crisis for the freshman football team: We didn't have enough players to compete. Only twenty kids came out for the first day of practice in August, two weeks before the start of school. We needed twenty-five players on the roster before we could take the field.

The coaching staff wasn't going to let something like a poor turnout get in our way, so they scrambled like a quarterback running out of the pocket and found us a half-dozen players. I'm not sure how they did it, but I didn't care. I was fired up to begin high school football, and six months of following Uncle Ariel's weight-training program had added new muscle to my frame. At the start of my freshman year, I was six feet, one inch tall and weighed just over two hundred pounds.

With such a small freshman squad, the coaches said I would be playing both ways: running back on offense and middle linebacker on defense. I was down with that. I liked to run over bodies and hit people.

We had more than a few guys playing football for the first time, so on the first day of practice, Coach Ben LaSala gathered all the players—from the freshman, JV, and varsity teams—around him. "Take a seat, everyone!" Coach yelled out, and the players obeyed by sitting down on the grass field. Barrel-chested with a buzz cut and in his early forties, Coach LaSala had been the Colonia varsity football coach for the last ten years, and his booming voice commanded respect.

"Gentlemen, I want you to find the warning sticker inside your helmet," said Coach LaSala.

I didn't know that football helmets came with warning stickers, but I found one attached to the plastic lining inside my helmet.

"Everyone find their sticker?" Coach LaSala asked.

"Good. Let's read it out loud together."

In unison, here is what we read:

WARNING: Keep your head up. Do not butt, ram, spear, or strike an opponent with any part of this helmet or face guard. This is a violation of football rules and may cause you to suffer severe brain or neck injury, including paralysis or death and possible injury to your opponent. Contact in football may result in a concussion/brain injury, which no helmet can prevent. Symptoms include: loss of consciousness or memory, dizziness, headache, nausea, or confusion. If you have symptoms, immediately stop and report them to your coach, trainer, and parents. Do not return to a game or contact until all symptoms are gone and you receive medical clearance. Ignoring this warning may lead to another and more serious or fatal brain injury. NO HELMET SYSTEM CAN PROTECT YOU FROM SERIOUS BRAIN AND/OR NECK INJURIES, INCLUDING PARALYSIS OR DEATH. TO AVOID THESE RISKS, DO NOT ENGAGE IN THE SPORT OF FOOTBALL.

That was pretty serious. But Coach LaSala wasn't done yet.

"Listen up, men. You know football is a dangerous sport. You have to be a tough guy to play football. This is not a natural game. People aren't born to come out banging heads with each other. That's why you tackle with your shoulder. You don't lead with your head. Don't put your head down, because when you don't keep your head up,

50

bad things can happen. When you tackle, I want you to tackle with your face up, not with your head down."

I had heard this type of speech before in Pop Warner, but it never hurt to have a refresher course. As we broke off to start our first drills of the season, Coach LaSala issued one more reminder to the team: "When you put your helmets on, strap them up and always keep your head up when you tackle."

Coach LaSala's words that day stayed with me for the rest of my football career. I understood the importance of keeping my chin up when making a tackle, but like any young teenager who thought he was invincible, I don't think it fully sunk in what a big risk I was taking by stepping onto a football field. All I knew at that time was that I loved the game, loved the contact, and loved winning. Nothing was going to get in my way.

I even liked the tackling drills. I'd break down into the football position, where my feet were shoulder-width apart and my knees were bent. Then I'd place my arms in the locked-and-loaded position with shoulders bent down, aiming at the target I wanted to hit.

If a runner came at me, I was taught to "bite the ball." I would put my face right on the ball as I wrapped up the player for the tackle. If I couldn't bite the ball, then I had to execute a "wrap and roll," which meant grabbing the legs and rolling with it. If I couldn't wrap and roll, then the tackle of last resort was diving for his legs and trying to trip up the runner or receiver by hitting his ankles.

But the main way to bring people down was to bite the ball. I got pretty good at exploding at my target, putting my face right on the ball, and driving my adversary to the ground. Aggression was the key, and the more speed you had at the point of impact, the more likely you'd make a stop and plant the ballcarrier to the turf.

The Birthplace of College Football

I celebrated my fourteenth birthday on Saturday, September 4, 2004, by going to a big home game between Rutgers University and Michigan State. I knew all about Rutgers, since the school was in my backyard—just twenty minutes away—and Mom had been a college student there, although not for long.

Rutgers fans hadn't had much to cheer about for years. Head coach Greg Schiano—pronounced *Shee-ah-no*—was starting his third season at Rutgers, and the team hadn't finished above .500 in eleven seasons. Truth be known: Rutgers had some pitiful years (0-11, 1-10, 2-9, and 3-8) during that stretch, but the 2003 season was a ray of sunshine: Rutgers had gone 5-7, lifting everyone's hopes that Coach Schiano had turned around the oldest college program in the nation.

Rutgers was known as the Birthplace of College Football, and the reason that's capitalized is because the first-ever intercollegiate football game was played on November 6, 1869, on a plot of land where the Rutgers gymnasium sits today. Princeton was the foe, and Rutgers won 6-4.

The Scarlet Knights, however, hadn't won that much since those post-Civil War days when the game more resembled rugby and players didn't wear helmets of any kind. When I was growing up, Rutgers had their hands full playing in the Big East conference against such rivals as Syracuse, Pittsburgh, West Virginia, Louisville, Cincinnati, and South Florida.

On this particular day, Michigan State was in town for the first game of the season, and Rutgers fans set a stadium record with 42,612 fans in attendance. The atmosphere was electric, and I wondered what it would be like to be one of those players. To run up and down that field, making plays, seemed like the coolest thing ever.

While exiting the stadium, I ran into Coach LaSala,

our high school varsity coach. "How about you come along for varsity practice on Monday? You wanna do that?" he asked after wishing me a happy birthday.

Of course, Coach.

But inside of me, my heart was beating fast. A freshman practicing—or possibly playing—with the varsity was a big deal. Maybe Coach wanted to see if I could handle the next level. Maybe I was being called up.

I showed up for practice on Monday, not sure what was going to happen. Well, nothing happened. The next day I was told to report for freshman team practice with no explanation about why I was returning to the freshman team. None of the coaches were talking.

It was back to playing both ways on the freshman team for me. We lost our first game to Monroe, but after that minor defeat, our team couldn't be stopped. We kept winning game after game. I was a force at running back, and I made plenty of stops from my middle linebacker position.

This was the first time I had ever played with guys my age, and I was enjoying myself because I was bigger and faster than my competition. Even better was winning all those games, which certainly made it easier to suit up for practice each afternoon.

We were really on a roll when Rob Starling, the starting middle linebacker on the varsity team, got hurt in the Spotswood game. Coach LaSala didn't have a backup middle linebacker, so he said he was bringing me up from the freshman team for the last three games of the season.

I was surprised by Coach's decision, since my "tryout" with the varsity earlier in the season had lasted only one day. We had no freshmen on the Colonia High varsity team—and only a handful in our league. But I believed I had ability, and I was certainly ready to give it a shot.

Even though I was eager to play, this was the most nervous I had ever been playing football. I had big shoes to fill. With only a few practices to learn the defense, the last thing I wanted to do was make a mistake and let my team down. In my first varsity game, I surprised myself—and my coaches—by making fifteen tackles. Then I followed up that effort with seventeen tackles in the second game. Finally, I was good for thirteen tackles in the third and final game of the season.

I truly had never played better in all three games. As the "quarterback" of the defense from my middle linebacker position, I was all over the field on every defensive play—pass or run. The coaches were amazed that I made so many clean tackles. Normally, ten tackles in a game is a lot. No one *averages* fifteen tackles a game.

I overheard Coach LaSala telling local reporters, "Where has this kid been all season? We could have won more games if we had LeGrand in our defensive backfield."

Even once I was playing basketball that winter and planned to get on the mound and play center field with the baseball team in the spring, I had a feeling that my future lay with football.

An Unexpected Pitch

As soon as the basketball season was over, it was baseball's turn. I played center field and pitched, just like in my Little League days. I could swing the bat, too: I had forty-seven home runs from ages eleven to thirteen, and I hit my share of dingers in freshman ball as well. The other way I helped out was by pitching. I had grown to six feet, two inches, and I was in the 215-pound range. I was a presence on the mound.

I'll never forget one game against South River on a cold, drizzly spring day. I was on the mound, whipping the ball in there, but I was a little wild. Maybe I was really wild. Maybe I was so wild that I was hitting batters right and left. I pinged three pitches off the helmets of three different South River players. The second time they batted against me, they were too scared to stand in the batter's box, so they gave me half the plate.

Coach LaSala teased me the rest of the season for hitting those three batters. "Looks like you got all those little South River kids scared of you after hitting them in the head with that ninety-mile-an-hour fastball of yours."

"My bad, Coach. I'm sorry." I had a grin on my face.

I didn't know it at the time, but when I'd started lifting in my basement, I was really starting to bulk up my upper chest, and that changed my pitching motion. My body subtly made changes to the way I threw based on the new and bigger muscles on my frame. No wonder I had my wild days out there.

What I didn't know then was that during the baseball season, the Rutgers football team was recruiting Shamar Graves, a wide receiver from Woodbridge High, one of our main rivals. The Rutgers coaches were looking at film of Shamar playing against Colonia, and they kept seeing this kid flying around and making tackles.

"Who's that?" asked one coach.

"Some freshman that Bennie LaSala likes at Colonia. He's something, isn't he?"

That bit of film changed my life.

The story I heard was that after the Rutgers coaches saw me perform on five plays, they decided to offer me a scholarship.

To a freshman. With three games of varsity experience.

I know. It all sounds rather unbelievable, and it was.

Here's what happened. Late in my freshman year, Mom was driving to work when her cell phone rang. Coach LaSala was on the phone.

"Are you sitting down?" he asked.

"Matter of fact, I'm in the car on my way to work," Mom said.

"Good, because I'm in the office with Joe Susan, one of the football coaches at Rutgers. He's here because he wants to offer Eric a full-ride scholarship."

Mom nearly drove off the road. The thought of not having to pay for my college education was just amazing. It was always going to be a tough road for a single mother, but now I would have the chance to go to a university, get a degree, and gain a better start on life.

Mom was practically hyperventilating. "I don't know what to say," my mother said after she caught her breath.

"Listen, Karen, Coach Susan is not supposed to have any contact with Eric because he's a freshman. Would you mind if I called Eric out of class to tell him myself?" Coach LaSala asked.

"Go ahead, Coach. I think he'll be thrilled."

I was in my Spanish I class when I got a message that Coach LaSala wanted to see me in his office. That was a strange request, especially coming in the morning.

I stepped into his office, and Coach LaSala asked me to close the door.

"Eric, Coach Joe Susan with the Rutgers football team drove over this morning from New Brunswick because he wants to offer you a scholarship to play football at Rutgers."

My jaw dropped.

"I know, you're just a freshman, but Coach Susan told me that you had made quite an impression on him and the Rutgers staff during your three games on varsity last season. He watched film on you and said you were all over the place making tackles. He said he couldn't imagine where you're going to be when you're a senior."

This was all happening so fast, but Coach LaSala wasn't finished. "Coach Susan can't contact you directly because of NCAA recruiting rules, but he wanted me to remind you that Coach Schiano is turning the Rutgers football program around. Even though the team was 4-7 last season, the foundation has been laid for better things. Rutgers football wants you to be part of that turnaround. Even though it's only verbal at this time, that's why Rutgers is willing to offer you a full scholarship and have you come play for the Scarlet Knights."

My world spun. I was still a ninth grader, a lowly freshman. The only thing I could mumble was, "Really?"

Coach LaSala smiled. "Right now, Rutgers cannot formally offer you a scholarship in writing until your junior year. At that time, you can only make a verbal commitment until National Signing Day your senior year, which is always the first Wednesday in February. It's important that you continue to maintain good grades until then, so I'm sure you'll be motivated to pay attention in class and keep studying."

I was still stunned. *What? Is this really like a dream coming true? This fast after only three games?*

"Wow, thank you very much for telling me," I said. "I really appreciate it." I really didn't know what I could or should say at this point.

Coach LaSala announced that the meeting was over.

"Congratulations, Eric, but you got to get back to class. Float yourself back on a cloud if you want."

News Travels Quick

After he shooed me out of the office, I was walking down the hall when I ran into a random guy, not even a close friend, and said, "Wow, Rutgers just offered me a scholarship to play football."

It didn't take long for the good news to blow up through the school, and I heard that Coach LaSala was crazy with joy, telling all the faculty. And not just that—news of the Rutgers preemptive offer also made its way around the recruiting circles. Within days, Al Golden, the defensive coordinator at the University of Virginia, called Coach LaSala and told him that he was upset that Virginia wasn't the first one to offer me a full ride. Other college football programs got wind of Rutgers's offer and said they wanted their chance as well.

We only had a week or two of baseball left, but after the thunderbolt from Rutgers, my heart wasn't in baseball anymore. It was nice to finish with a winning season as we compiled a 17-10 record, but after the last out was recorded, I knew I was hanging up my mitt. I was done with baseball and done with basketball. From then on, football would become my life, and I would do whatever it took to make myself a better player. All I wanted to do was lift, work out, and get stronger.

I lifted with my team all that summer in our weight room at Colonia High. The weight set that Mom had purchased for me the previous Christmas gathered dust in the basement. She was pretty upset about it and ended up selling my weights to one of my friends a few years later, but I needed the camaraderie and accountability that came with lifting with my teammates.

I was bulking up with a real football player's build. By the end of the summer, I could clean-and-jerk 225 pounds, and on the bench I improved from 185 to 275 pounds. Coach LaSala told the local newspaper that I was a "freak of nature, a big-time player."

Hearing that gave me a lot of confidence, just as it did knowing that Rutgers wanted me to play for them when I was done with high school. I attended the Rutgers summer football camp, where I met Coach Schiano for the first time and was greatly impressed with his energy and leadership. Each summer, nearly every Division I school holds a summer camp for high school players, which is a good way to improve your football skills but also a good way to showcase your abilities.

During the four-day camp, you get separated into position groups and then work with the position coaches. This was not a full-contact camp—players weren't even allowed to bring helmets. We ran through drills and seven-on-seven scrimmages in T-shirts, shorts, and football cleats.

I did the running back and linebacker drills, and every now and then one of the position coaches would pull me off to the side and talk to me. It wasn't so much about what was happening on the field but "How are you doing?" and "Are you liking it here?"—stuff like that. That's how the recruiting process works, getting players familiar with their way and forming relationships. You get a look at them, and they get a look at you.

For many of the players like me, this was our first time in a college setting. We stayed in the athletic dorm, where the nights got pretty crazy. There were kids running around and throwing baby powder on other people's doors or tossing water balloons around the halls. We were having tons of fun being on our own. I wasn't homesick at all.

Coach LaSala's son, Joe, who was in the same class as

me, was there, but Joe had been attending South River. He told me and my teammate Nate Brown that he was transferring to Colonia so he could join our team and be coached by his father, but he wanted to keep the news on the down low. So no one knew—or was supposed to know.

One night, our Colonia crew was hanging out in the commons with the South River crew, and Nate said in front of everybody, "So, Joey, I hear you're transferring to Colonia next year."

Immediate silence. And then Joe, with the straightest face ever, said, "I don't know what you're talking about."

Meanwhile, I'm punching Nate in the shoulder and telling him to shut up. But now the word was out, thanks to Nate's loose lips, and there was nothing we could do about it.

Two months later, Joe and his family moved into our school district, and Joe played wide receiver on our team. Today, Joey LaSala is one of my very best friends.

5

THE LETTERS NEVER STOP

I COULDN'T WAIT FOR my first full season of varsity football to start. Once again, on the first day of August practice, Coach LaSala gathered us around for an important announcement. "Gentlemen, take off your helmets and look at what the warning sticker says inside." Then Coach asked us to read the warning label all together out loud, which we did.

> WARNING: Keep your head up. Do not butt, ram, spear, or strike an opponent with any part of this helmet or . . .

"Very good, guys," Coach LaSala said when we were done. "The reason why I have you guys read the warning label every year is because it's super important. You have to keep your head up when you tackle. Bad things happen when you lead with the head, so don't use your helmet as a battering ram. You'll get hurt, perhaps severely injured. Instead, remember to bite the ball and play solid, hard-nosed football the Patriot way."

He was right about the hard-nosed football part. I was on the receiving end of one of those hits when I took my most colossal hit ever during my sophomore year. It happened during a game against Carteret High, when I gathered in a screen pass. I thought I had a couple of linemen out in the flat with me, but I guess I didn't, because their strong-side defensive end, Jason Adjepong Worilds, leveled me with a thundering shot that nailed me to the ground like a stake. I was shook up pretty bad and had no idea what was going on after that collision. (Jason was an All-Stater who went on to Virginia Tech and wound up being a second-round draft pick of the Pittsburgh Steelers in 2010, where he's now part of the Steel Curtain defense. Good luck, NFL.)

Most of the time, though, I was making good yardage

with the ball in my hands and delivering my own Worilds-like shots from the linebacker position. I was more than holding my own out there on the field. My coaches were pleased with how I was playing and decided to move me from fullback (the guy who usually blocks) to halfback (the guy who's getting the handoff from the quarterback and expected to churn out big yards to keep the offense moving).

I had some big games, like against South Plainfield when I ran for 216 yards on thirty-six carries—a six-yards-per-carry average—to help us win our first game of the season. I also recorded eleven tackles, including a "signature hit"—which is how the local newspaper described my body slam on running back Jamar Beverly. It was sure better pile-driving a runner to the ground than being on the receiving end of such a big hit.

Coach LaSala sang my praises to any reporter who would listen. "Eric is unbelievable," he told one local newspaper. "He's the best fifteen-year-old I've ever seen. He won't outrun you, but he'll barrel over you. We recently moved Eric to halfback. We're not going to be fancy anymore. We're just going to give him the ball. Eric is a big-time player. If there's someone out there better than him at his age, I'd like to see him."

Letters Filling the Mailbox

Because of my strong play, recruiting letters started flowing into our Avenel mailbox from dozens of college football programs. Big-name programs such as Notre Dame; Big Ten schools like Michigan, Michigan State, and Ohio State; such Southeastern Conference schools as Alabama, Florida, and Tennessee; and every Big East school that played in Rutgers's conference were flooding my mailbox with letters and slick promotional material.

A lot of trees must have been cut down, because there were days when I received fifteen letters or brochures. It was ridiculous. Some programs sent me a letter every day for a week or two at a time. (I guess that's nothing: Alvin Kamara, a tailback from Georgia scheduled to graduate from high school in 2013, received 105 letters from the University of Alabama in *one day!*)

I didn't open every letter, especially those from schools that sent me two, three, four, or sometimes five pieces of mail each week. It wasn't that I was ungrateful, but I didn't have time with school, practice, homework, and playing games.

We had a so-so year my sophomore season, finishing 5-5, which qualified us for the state playoffs and a matchup against Middletown South, the No. 1 seed in the state playoffs for our division. They were huge. They were gigantic. They had three players who went on to Division 1 programs at Stanford, Georgia, and Lehigh. We got destroyed, 52–26, and it could have been worse.

In terms of stats, though, I had a great year: 1,064 yards rushing (or a little more than a hundred yards per game) and 109 tackles (or a little more than ten per game). I also ran my fastest forty-yard dash ever—a 4.71. That's about where you want to be to chase down fast running backs. For the rest of my football career, I'd be in the 4.7s, which is excellent for a linebacker but a little slow for what coaches want to see out of their running backs.

Even though I could be a dominant halfback at the high school level, I knew my future was on the defensive side of the ball in college football. The Rutgers coaches were telling me that I would be playing linebacker, which sounded great to me. Something about chasing down a runner and stopping him cold gave me a bigger rush than playing running back.

True to what Coach Susan said to Coach LaSala at the end of my freshman year, Rutgers *did* offer me, in writing, a full-ride football scholarship on September 1, as promised.

Sure, it was a piece of paper, but Rutgers's scholarship offer in writing represented a lot more to me—a momentous opportunity to have my college education paid for and to play football on a big stage.

Pandemonium in Piscataway

At the start of my junior season in 2006, things were really looking up at Rutgers. Coach Schiano had guided the Scarlet Knights to their first winning season in fourteen years in 2005 and only the second bowl game in Rutgers's 136-year history of playing football. Even fair-weather Rutgers fans were jumping on the bandwagon again.

The scholarship offer from Rutgers was certainly greeted with enthusiasm by Mom and me, but we were not ready to give our verbal agreement during my junior season. Too many other teams wanted me to play for them, so we thought we'd let things settle a bit and see what developed.

But then Rutgers kept winning. And winning. And winning. Going into the ninth game of the season, the Scarlet Knights were *undefeated* at 8-0, and next up was a home game against the Louisville Cardinals, who were the No. 3 team in the country at 7–1 and coming off a big victory over highly regarded West Virginia.

I just *had* to be there at Rutgers Stadium with my buddies, and I'm sure glad I went. It was a really great game played on a Thursday night before a national audience looking in on ESPN. The outcome wasn't decided until Jeremy Ito kicked a tiebreaking twenty-eight-yard field goal with thirteen seconds left to give Rutgers a 28–25 lead.

When Devraun Thompson sacked Louisville quarterback Brian Brohm on the last play of the game, I was among the tens of thousands of crazy fans who stormed the field to celebrate. "It's pandemonium in Piscataway," exclaimed Rutgers Radio play-by-play announcer Chris Carlin while I danced on the field with my buddies and slapped the shoulder pads of the victors. In the happiness of that cool evening, I imagined that one day I, too, would be part of an awesome scene like this. (A little geography lesson: Rutgers Stadium is located in Piscataway, while most of the Rutgers campus is situated in New Brunswick.)

"Keep chopping!" was the mantra at Rutgers, because Coach Schiano, while prowling the sidelines, would slam the edge of his right hand into the palm of his left in a chopping motion. All season long Coach Schiano had been preaching the phrase "Keep chopping" to his players. He wanted the players to imagine that they were in a forest all by themselves, but they each had an ax in their hands. "You take your time chopping down one tree," Coach Schiano said, "and when that tree falls, you take a breath and then you go on to the next one. Football is just like that. It doesn't matter whether you're on offense, defense, or special teams, you keep chopping, taking each play one at a time. When you win that battle, you go on to the next. You chop, chop, chop all game long, and eventually you'll come out of the forest with a victory."

"Keep chopping!" was a great motivational metaphor that tapped into the ebb and flow of football games: You have to keep plugging away, never giving up. Since victory often doesn't come until the very end in football, at least not until the last seconds tick off, you have to continue "chopping" until success is assured.

Unfortunately, Colonia High wasn't experiencing the same level of success as Rutgers. We started the season with high hopes, and I was amazed when Coach LaSala made me a team captain as a junior—the first time that had ever happened in Colonia High history.

Even though my teammates and I had all the motivation in the world, we finished my junior season with a 3-7 record, which was a huge disappointment. But since I had my biggest year as a linebacker with 150 tackles, or fifteen per game, the cards and letters kept arriving in our mailbox each day. Dozens of schools wanted me to visit on official recruiting trips.

Even though I was loyal to Rutgers, Mom and I decided that I should look at some out-of-state schools just to be sure. I took recruiting trips to the University of Maryland, the University of Virginia, and the University of Notre Dame during and after my junior season. I made plans to visit the University of Florida, Florida State University, and the University of Miami in the fall of my senior year—all great schools with great football programs. The Miami Hurricanes were my favorite college team growing up, because I used to choose the 'Canes as my team whenever I played the NCAA Football video game on my PlayStation.

What was I looking for in a school? For starters, I wanted an excellent education, but I was also looking for a great family atmosphere with the coaches and the football program. Lastly, I was looking for a place where I could develop my skills as a football player. After that, it was a matter of weighing the intangibles, like the distance from home or the academic program in place for the football players. Each school I visited had its own characteristics—and its own pluses and minuses. The trick was finding the school that best matched my needs and my desires to play football at a major college program.

As it turned out, though, there was a bit more to it than that: I also needed to prove myself academically before I'd get my chance to play.

The Dreaded SAT

All the full-ride scholarship offers I received from these great schools had one contingency attached to them: I had to score at least a 910 on my SATs. That seemed quite doable. I had always been a "good" student even though I had been diagnosed with ADHD—attention-deficit/hyperactivity disorder—back in second grade.

I used to go to the bathroom a lot back in elementary school, raising my hand four or five times a day to ask my teacher if I could please, please use the hall pass. Mom noticed that whenever we'd be in the car for more than an hour, I'd ask her to pull over for a pit stop, too. Same thing at the movies—sometimes I would even go twice during a film. But if I was playing a Pop Warner game or a baseball game, I never had to go.

Prompted by a note from my second-grade teacher informing Mom that she had a son who was constantly going to the bathroom during the school day, Mom decided something needed to be done. She took me to a doctor who determined that, plumbing-wise, everything was fine. He referred me to my pediatrician, who gave Mom a questionnaire to fill out. Based on those answers, I was diagnosed with ADHD because I could not sit still, pay attention in class, or keep my focus on my schoolwork.

The treatment protocol was to put me on an anti-depressant like Ritalin or Adderall. These drugs were supposed to make me mellow out and become more docile and obedient.

Mom wasn't big on medications unless absolutely necessary. She had heard stories of kids diagnosed with ADHD or attention deficit disorder who would sit in the classroom like zombies. That was not what she wanted for me.

But there was some pressure on her to do *something*. She finally said she would agree to put me on antidepressant medications, as long as it was a very low, low dose and not Ritalin, which she felt was too strong.

So I was put on a low dose of Adderall, just five milligrams, which I suppose did help me pay more attention in school and calm me down a bit. But Mom and my teachers had to stay on top of me to do my schoolwork, because I was never that good at keeping track of all my assignments.

"What do you have for homework tonight?" Mom would ask.

"I don't know," I would reply.

"Did you bring home your books?"

"I forgot."

We had these conversations so many times, and Mom told me I had to do better and do something different. She went to my teacher, and together they came up with a plan where I had to present my notebook to my teacher at the end of the day. Inside that notebook was a chart of everything I needed to do that evening and that week. And that's what we generally did from second grade all the way up to eighth grade.

I think I just needed more structure. Mom learned that she had to stay on top of me, and because she put in that extra effort, I got a lot more education than I would have otherwise.

Meanwhile, Mom never changed my dose of Adderall

throughout elementary school and middle school. As I entered Colonia High, I told Mom that I didn't want to take Adderall anymore. I felt the medication made me unsociable, like I didn't want to be bothered with people, which was totally against my outgoing nature. I always viewed myself as a very social person who was popular with my peers. Everyone loved me, and I loved everyone around me.

"Okay, if you can do your work, and if you feel like you can keep up and your grades don't slip, I have no problem with you stopping the medication," she said.

So I stopped. There were no adverse reactions. I stayed on top of my schoolwork. My grades were okay at Colonia: lots of Bs and Cs. But to take advantage of a football scholarship, I needed a decent SAT score, and sitting in a chair for more than three hours on a Saturday morning wasn't my strong suit. I was not a great test taker . . . or even a good one.

I will admit to feeling pretty nervous when I sat down for my first SAT midway through my junior year. The motivation was there. I concentrated hard for nearly four hours, and when the test was over, I set my No. 2 lead pencil down. I hoped I had done well enough.

When the results came back, I learned that I had

received a score of 1060. I made it! A 1060 is better than 910, right?

I texted Coach Urban Meyer at the University of Florida—the Gators wanted me, too—with the good news. I texted Charlie Weis at Notre Dame, and coaches at a bunch of other schools, telling them that I qualified academically. I received replies congratulating me and saying they'd be faxing me a scholarship offer in the morning.

Then Coach LaSala got wind of what I had done and called me into his office. "Eric, you didn't make it," he announced. "You got a 790 on the first two parts, Mathematics and Critical Reading. The 1060 was for all three parts, including the Writing section."

Ooh. That wasn't good news.

"But Coach, I just texted all those coaches that I'm qualified. And now ..."

"Don't worry about it. I'll handle everything. Bottom line is you didn't make it, so we'll have to keep working at it."

I was devastated by this news. *Are you kidding me? Can I be that dumb?*

Maybe I'd had a bad day. I signed up for the next SAT, but I showed only a slight improvement, moving the bar from 790 to 830. Then I tried the ACT, but that was a disaster, too.

A worried Coach LaSala contacted my mother to come in and talk about what to do. We had a major problem on our hands. As of right now, my scholarship offers and dreams of playing college football at a four-year school were ruined if I didn't get my SAT score up. I wasn't going anywhere except a junior college with an 830.

Coach LaSala recommended that we bite the bullet and put me in an SAT tutor program, but he said that could be costly. Mom called around and didn't like the vibes from several learning centers, but she clicked with the person at the Princeton Review, which had a program where they would send a tutor to our house. It was a bit more expensive this way, but Mom thought I'd do better in a one-on-one setting rather than a class atmosphere.

The cost: $2,800.

Mom was a single parent, so this was a lot of money for us. I tried to tell her it was too much to pay, that I'd do better next time, that I'd try my hardest, but she was insistent, saying that if $2,800 got my college education paid for, then it would all be worth it. She put the large fee on her credit card, and off we went.

My tutor was awesome. She came twice a week to my house after school (I wasn't playing basketball or baseball) and worked with me for two months during the spring of my junior year.

I had to get up early to take the SAT that Saturday morning in April; I was prepared for battle. When Mom dropped me off, she looked me in the eyes. "Oh God, good luck," she said.

I needed the prayer because I had to do well.

Two weeks later, I received the results at school, and the numbers set off some whooping and hollering in the hallways. I got an 1190 on Mathematics and Critical Reading, an increase of 400 points, or more than 50 percent, from my first attempt, and a 1650 on all three SATs, an increase of more than 55 percent from my first test.

"Maybe I should go to Harvard," I joked to Mom.

This time I didn't text any coaches, fulfilling my vow of never doing that again. But I did text Coach LaSala, and he replied, "Amazing! This is great news!"

It was really great news.

Recruiting Visitors

As word got out that I was eligible for a scholarship, coaches from more and more programs came to Colonia

High to visit me. It felt like every other day I was getting called out of class.

I was on my way back from a bathroom break from chemistry class one morning—well, a prolonged bathroom break that included a long, long stop to sample some of the fresh chocolate chip cookies from the cooking class—when I saw my chemistry teacher running after me. "Eric, you have to get to the guidance office now! Some coach from Penn State is waiting for you there."

I did a U-turn and sprinted to the guidance office, where a perturbed Coach LaSala was cooling his heels. He got in my face and said, "I'm going to jack you up!"

I backed up to the wall as he advanced on me, wondering what I had done wrong.

"Where have you been?" he demanded. "I had half my health class looking for you."

"I was in the cooking room, Coach."

"What were you doing in the cooking room? You were supposed to be in—"

A smile formed on Coach LaSala's lips. "Oh, I know. Making sure the cookies weren't poisoned, right?"

I looked around the guidance room, and the other counselors had their heads down. Coach LaSala calmed down and led me to a nearby conference room, where a

Penn State football coach had been waiting patiently to see me. He had been told that I was home sick but that I was on my way in to see him.

I survived that morning, even though I thought Coach was going to kill me. But I almost didn't survive the glare I received from Charlie Weis when he dropped by Colonia High to talk to Coach LaSala about me. The Notre Dame head coach was a larger-than-life figure, even for someone who had undergone gastric bypass surgery and had lost some weight after tipping the scales at 350 pounds.

Well, word got around school that Charlie Weis was coming. "Coach Weis was very specific," Coach LaSala said. "He said he didn't want anything crazy going on when he gets here."

"Got it," I replied.

Coach's smartphone buzzed. "I'm here" was the message from Coach Weis.

A long, sleek black limousine with tinted windows rolled up to the school entrance.

Coach was approaching the car when two students rushed up to him, clutching pieces of paper. "Can we have your autograph?" one of them said as Coach Weis stepped out of the limo.

More students started to head over, but Coach LaSala shooed them away. Our principal was waiting inside, and the next thing you know, pictures were being taken of Coach LaSala, our principal, and Charlie Weis seated at the table, with Coach Weis's huge Super Bowl ring clearly visible on his right hand. He had won four of them over the years, coaching for the New York Giants and New England Patriots.

Apparently, this was an "unofficial visit," so Coach Weis had to "talk" to me through my coach. So he'd look at Coach LaSala and say things like, "I think Eric would really like coming to Notre Dame" and "Tell Eric that our recruiting class is rated in the top ten."

Rules are rules, and rules are a big deal with college football coaches.

Decision Time

Late one afternoon in May, I received a phone call from Coach Schiano. We made the usual small talk, and then he got down to business.

"Eric, we have been recruiting you since your freshman year, and we have been by your side through everything. We really want you to come and play here at Rutgers. We had a big season last year. We were 11-2 and ranked No. 12 in the nation. We want you to come be a part of the excitement at Scarlet Nation, so now we need to know where your head is at. Have you made a decision? Can we count on you coming to Rutgers in the summer of 2008?"

I needed to scramble out of the pocket. "Coach, can I call you back?"

He said that was fine, and Coach reminded me that he was available for any questions I might have.

I hung up and thought about how Rutgers had been with me through this whole recruiting thing. They were always my number one. They made me an offer as a freshman, they were close to home, and I had been on campus a hundred times. There was a family atmosphere, and I believed that Coach Schiano and his assistants honestly cared about me as a person and as a football player.

I called Mom and told her about the phone call from Coach Schiano. We knew this call was coming sooner or later, and now it looked like things were coming to a head. "Mom, I'm thinking about committing myself to Rutgers."

"Are you sure?" she asked. "Is this really where you want to go?"

I exhaled a deep breath. "I believe Rutgers is where I want to go. You can go to all my home games, and I'd be close to home. They've recruited me from day one."

I could hear my mother relax on the other end of the phone. "If you want to go to Rutgers, I'll be more than happy," she said.

"Good. Let me call Coach Schiano back."

Just five minutes had passed when I reached Coach Schiano. I didn't waste any time. "Coach, I've made my decision. I'm coming to Rutgers."

Once again, I heard an adult say, "Are you sure?"

"Yes, I'm sure."

There was a pause. "So you're telling me that you're giving me your word. Only men give their word and really mean it and keep it."

"Coach, I'm giving you my word. I know I might be a young man, but I'm giving you my word that I'm coming to Rutgers. And I'm not changing my mind."

I heard an exhale of relief on the line. "Then Eric LeGrand, let me be the first to welcome you to Rutgers University. Congratulations. You are now part of the Rutgers football family."

Then Coach put his phone on speaker, and it was apparent that he was in his office or a conference room, because several Rutgers coaches hollered their congratulations. That just confirmed in my heart that I had made the right choice.

Over the next few weeks, and right through my senior season, coaches from Virginia, Michigan, and Michigan State contacted Coach LaSala to make their pitch with me, but he said I had committed to Rutgers and that decision was firm. I was so gung-ho for Rutgers that I started recruiting *my* friends—the ones I had met at the Rutgers summer camps—to come join me in Piscataway. I got Scott Vallone from Long Island and Art Forst from Manasquan, New Jersey, to commit. It was shaping up to be a great freshman class at Rutgers, but I still had some unfinished business at Colonia High.

Finishing Strong

We had an excellent turnaround on the field my senior year, winning seven of ten games and capturing our first Greater Middlesex Conference White Division championship since 1999. You could tell Rutgers was on my mind when we defeated a tough South Plainfield team in double overtime, 10-7. "We just kept coming back, kept chopping the whole game," I told a reporter from the *Star-Ledger*. I'm sure Coach Schiano was smiling.

I ran well my senior year, gaining 970 yards. On the defensive side, my preseason goal was 200 tackles, but I collected only 112 as teams tried to run away from me. I also played a third position—quarterback—which takes a little explaining.

Our conference championship qualified us for the state championship playoffs, with a first-round matchup against Scotch Plains-Fanwood High School. Our senior-heavy team had been ballin' it all season long, and the feeling in the locker room was *This is our year.*

Before the game, Coach LaSala pulled me aside. "I've got good news and bad news," he said. "The bad news is Jordan Edmonds can't start. The good news is that you know all the plays, so you're going to play quarterback tonight."

I gulped. I knew that our quarterback hadn't been feeling well all week, and during the pregame meal Jordan sipped Pepto-Bismol instead of eating with the rest of the team. But I had all the confidence in the world that I could quarterback this team to victory.

First down on offense, I dropped back and hit my friend Nate Brown on a post route, good for twelve yards. Then I had to roll out to escape a blitz. As I headed toward the sideline, looking for an open receiver, the ball fell out of my hand. I watched helplessly as the ball bounced out-of-bounds, which was good news for us because we retained possession. It struck me that maybe playing quarterback wasn't as easy as I'd thought.

On my next pass, I was going long the entire way. I saw Cory Jacik streaking down the sideline. It looked like he had a step or two on his man, so I chucked the ball up there, sixty yards in the air. I must have put too much oomph under the throw, because their cornerback intercepted the ball.

After three series, Coach LaSala had seen enough. He inserted a pale-looking Jordan Edmonds back into the game, and he threw five INTs. In all, we had eight turnovers and lost by six points, 19-13.

I was devastated. We should have easily won that game. I felt like we were definitely the better team, but the turnovers killed us. After the final seconds ticked off, I sat on the ground and let my body shake. I didn't cry, but I couldn't stop my body from shaking uncontrollably. I felt responsible for the loss because I had let my team down. Our state championship dreams were shattered.

We had one more game left—our annual rivalry game against Woodbridge High, which was always played the Saturday after Thanksgiving. Coach LaSala did a great job of keeping our spirits high after the letdown against Scotch Plains-Fanwood.

We dressed for the Saturday morning game in our locker room at Colonia High before boarding a bus for the ride over to Woodbridge High. As a senior, I knew this was it—my last game in a high school uniform. We were playing for the bragging rights trophy against our crosstown rivals, so this was our chance to finish strong.

Leaving the locker room, I passed under the door, where a sign was attached just above the transom. In big black block letters, it said:

BELIEVE

My teammates jumped up and tapped that sign as they exited the locker room, a ritual that bonded us together before every game. *Believe* was our motto. We had to *believe* that we would play well and win. There was power in the conviction of things not yet seen.

For the last time as a Colonia High football player, I jumped up and tapped the sign with my left hand, slapping my fingers on the EL . . . for my initials, E.L., for Eric LeGrand.

We won my final game of high school football against Woodbridge High, but little did I know that BELIEVE would come to mean something completely different for me at Rutgers University.

6

NEW BEGINNING IN NEW BRUNSWICK

I DON'T THINK COACH Schiano and the Rutgers staff were too concerned that I might break my verbal commitment to sign a letter of intent on National Signing Day, not after they watched me play an earlier game against New Brunswick High.

We were playing a bigger, more established program when Coach Schiano, along with his assistants Joe Susan and Bob Fraser, came to our game that Friday night. I noticed they were standing in the back of the end zone, so when I scored on a running play, I kept on heading toward them and did some chopping right in front of their noses. Just a couple of real quick chops, though, so I wouldn't get a penalty. Then I stormed off the field and celebrated with my teammates. We ended up beating New Brunswick that night, too.

After I signed my National Letter of Intent in early February, I asked Coach if I could work out at the Hale Center on the Rutgers campus every day after school. I could, he replied, as long as I did my own weight-training program and didn't have any contact with the team or any of the coaches since I wasn't officially enrolled yet.

I was impressed by the Hale Center, which was the home of the Scarlet Knights' training, administrative, and academic resource facilities. The shiny place was state-of-the-art, complete with a game room featuring plush leather couches, flat-screen TVs, and pool tables. The massive and well-appointed weight room wasn't shabby either.

My school day was over at eleven a.m. my senior year, so I worked out a routine with my grandmother and mother so I could lift at Rutgers. Nana would pick me up from school and hand me two turkey burgers on wheat bread, since I wanted to drop ten pounds and get down to 230—a good weight for a linebacker. That's why I was on a diet of turkey burgers, which I would eat on our way to nearby Clark, where Mom worked.

My grandmother had to drive to Mom's place of work because that was where our only car was parked. Since I didn't have my own wheels—we couldn't afford a second car—I picked up Mom's well-used 1996 Honda Accord and drove it to Rutgers, where I worked out during the afternoon, returning in time to pick her up when she was finished for the day.

Only weeks after my senior prom, I enrolled at Rutgers. Because the Rutgers football program expected all players to attend summer school and participate in preseason weight training, I had to report at Rutgers on Tuesday, June 24, 2008. Colonia High, however, was holding their commencement exercises two days later, on June 26. This meant, technically speaking, that I attended Rutgers University without a high school diploma for forty-eight hours.

I'll admit that I felt a little grown up being a "college student" while I walked with the class of '08 wearing my cobalt-blue graduation gown. When I saw Mom beaming in the bleachers as I received my diploma, I was pumped. I knew a bright future awaited me at Rutgers. While it was sad to say good-bye to my high school friends and teammates, I knew I'd stay in touch with many of them. I was hoping they'd come to my games at Rutgers Stadium.

New Position

I adapted well to the new routine of college and had no problems. Mom wasn't emotional at all when I left home, because I was so close and came back every weekend.

During the week, I lived with the Rutgers football team in Metzger Hall, a four-story redbrick dorm on Busch Campus with eighteen-by-twelve-foot rooms. Metzger was where the athletic department housed athletes from various sports during the summer "bridge" program, which was mandatory for football players as well as the young men and women playing on the basketball teams. I had a great summer getting to know the guys on the football team before training camp started in early August.

Life was fairly simple. I would wake up, have breakfast, attend a writing class, and then work out at the Hale Center. Many afternoons, the players would arrange games called "seven-on-sevens," which are T-shirt-and-shorts, no-contact scrimmages involving seven offensive players against seven defensive players. Since I was going to be a linebacker at Rutgers, I ran around covering running backs coming out of the backfield.

The seven-on-sevens were student-run, because NCAA rules didn't allow coaches to run any preseason workouts until the start of training camp. When training camp finally opened the first week of August, I stopped by the equipment room to pick up my gear and choose a jersey number. At Colonia High, I had worn number 30 because Terrell Davis, a running back for the Denver Broncos back in my Pop Warner days, played with number 30 across his orange jersey. I loved the way TD ran the ball, and he was my favorite player growing up. In fact, the Broncos were my favorite NFL team, even though the New York Jets and New York Giants played in my backyard. From Pop Warner to varsity football at Colonia High, I wore number 30, a number that worked for a running back and linebacker.

In college and pro football, though, number 30 wasn't a linebacker number, so I chose number 52, because I was a huge fan of Ray Lewis, the ferocious middle linebacker for the Baltimore Ravens, who was a Pro Bowl lock every year. The dude was the best sideline-to-sideline player in football. He always got his man.

I was putting away my new jerseys and equipment when linebackers coach Bob Fraser approached me shortly after check-in. "Coach wants to see you in his office," he said.

That didn't sound good. What had I done?

"Have a seat, Eric," Coach Schiano said after I arrived.

I accepted his direction and waited for him to speak.

"You're probably wondering why you're here," he began, which elicited a nod from me. "I've been giving this some thought, and I'd like to move you from linebacker to defensive tackle. I think that you'll be better suited there."

After a spring of dieting to get down to my ideal weight—and eating Nana's turkey burgers—I was down to 232 pounds. That was a lean-and-mean weight for any college linebacker. But now Coach was talking about putting me on the defensive line, where I'd be matched up against guys who had a good fifty-, sixty-, or even seventy-pound weight advantage on me. They'd be able to push me around pretty good.

"Really, Coach?"

"With the experience we have at linebacker, you

probably wouldn't help us out this year at all," Coach Schiano said. "We want you to help us on the defensive line rotation. We believe you'll be a natural on the line."

In the trenches, he meant. The line of scrimmage was a war zone. Hand-to-hand combat. Gouging, kicking, and even punching. On the defensive line, you got down into a three-point stance every play, and when the ball was snapped, you were banging heads with giant offensive linemen.

Playing on the line was not at all glamorous compared to being a linebacker, who roams around freely and has the responsibility of tackling runners who burst through the line or dropping back into coverage. Linebackers learn to "read" where the quarterback is going to throw and have the opportunity to make interceptions, which often change the complexity of a game.

"There's another thing we'd like you to do for us," Coach Schiano continued. "We think you'd make a great special teams player."

I had played on special teams before—the units that are on the field during kicking plays. At Colonia High, I was part of the kickoff return team and liked blocking for our return guy.

"We pride ourselves on our special teams at Rutgers,"

Coach Schiano said. "The fans might not know it, but special teams decide ball games. You can put your opponent in bad field position, and you can take your team out of bad field position. Knowing your role and sacrificing your ego is a key component of successful special teams play, and we think you buy into that philosophy here at Rutgers."

What could I say except, "Sure, Coach. I'll do whatever you ask of me." Although the news that my days as a linebacker were over didn't thrill me, I had always been a team player.

I had second thoughts, though, after I told one of my teammates, Marvin Booker, about Coach's plans. "No, you gotta go up there, E," he said, meaning that I should request a meeting with Coach Schiano. "You tell him that you want to be a linebacker and don't belong down in the trenches."

Well, I didn't think I could tell Coach Schiano that he had made a mistake and should play me at linebacker, because that would be bordering on insubordination. But I did get the nerve to ask him if I could try out being a defensive tackle for a few days and, if I didn't like it, then we could talk about returning me to the linebacker position.

"Sure, we'll see how it goes," Coach Schiano said.

Once I started playing on the line, the coaching staff kept me there. In fact, I never played a down at the linebacker position during my college career at Rutgers.

Moving Around the Line

I really bonded with my teammates during the summer. After training camp opened, we went to a Navy Seals leadership conference and did other team-building exercises. Coach Schiano had everyone wear black bracelets with the letters F.A.M.I.L.Y., which meant "Forget About Me, I Love You"—another motto to go with "Keep chopping." Coach wore the rubber bracelet, too.

When the regular school year started in September, I moved into the Silvers Apartments, also on Busch Campus, which featured "garden-style" two-bedroom units with a living room, full kitchen, bath, and storage room. I roomed with Brandon Jones, a freshman defensive back and cornerback. Marquis Hamm, a defensive end, and Timothy Wright, a wide receiver, shared the other bedroom.

I didn't have to worry about my weight any longer, because now my goal was to *add* bulk. Good-bye, turkey burgers, hello, Hot Pockets. Even though the decision that

Coach wanted to play me on the defensive line was a blow, the good news was that he didn't want to redshirt me and sit me out a year before I could take the field. Just like in eighth grade when I initially weighed too much to play Pop Warner, I couldn't imagine going an entire season without playing football.

Playing against 300-pound offensive tackles and guards was an eye-opener during practice sessions. When they grabbed me at 232 pounds, it was like they owned me. Some of them threw me around like a Raggedy Ann doll. I had to be quick and fast, more nimble, which fit into Coach Schiano's defensive philosophy—small, swift, speedy, and strong.

I decided to keep number 52, even though I was moving to the defensive line, where players usually wore numbers in the seventies or nineties. No one on the Rutgers staff said anything about it, so I went with it.

We lost five out of our first six games, which caused a few panic buttons to be pushed at the Hale Center. Coach Schiano didn't like the way our fullbacks were playing, so he announced that he was moving me over to fullback for a tryout.

Fullback, like defensive lineman, was another head-banging position where your role is to be the lead blocker for your tailback or halfback. I was fine with grunt work, though. Anything to help the team.

After a couple of weeks, though, I discovered that playing fullback at the Division I level was a concussion waiting to happen. In practice, you're running into people and banging heads all the time. I was concerned, wondering how much punishment my body could take every single day. I soldiered on and did see action against UConn—the University of Connecticut—as well as Pittsburgh, so the coaching staff liked the way I was blocking.

But I was never handed the ball. You had to earn the ball in our program, and the coaching staff was certainly in no mood to hand the ball to a freshman. So I blocked as ferociously as I could and did a good job. After a handful of games, though, I was moved back to defensive end, which was fine with me. I was glad to no longer be a battering ram.

With all the movement between positions, what I was really sinking my teeth into was special teams. There are five special teams on every squad: kickoff, kickoff return, punt, punt return, and field goal unit. I was tapped for kickoff and kickoff return.

I especially liked playing on the kickoff team. I loved sprinting down the field, reading my keys—looking for how their kickoff team had set up for the return—and then finding the ball. I loved taking some guy out, whether it was a blocker or the return man.

A big hit can really fire up your team—and your fans. Mom remembers the time when we played the University of Pittsburgh midway through my freshman season at Heinz Field—home of the Pittsburgh Steelers. Mom couldn't afford to go to every out-of-town game, so she was watching the game with friends and family at a sports bar near the Rutgers campus. During a Rutgers kickoff, she watched me fly down the field and flatten the ballcarrier right after he caught the ball. Bam!

"That's my son!" she exclaimed as she slapped hands with friends.

What an adrenaline rush when our kicker, Teddy Dellaganna, sent the ball into the air, especially at the beginning of a game. I viewed the opening kickoff as a way to put our stamp on the game. If I made a huge hit, then I got our crowd into it immediately. If I got the crowd into the game, then they'd holler like crazy during the first set of downs. If we made a three-and-out stop, then the opposing team would have to punt from deep in their territory. The momentum would be all on our side, especially if our offense mounted a scoring drive.

I wanted to be the tone-setter. I wanted to be that guy. I wanted to get every Rutgers fan into the game—home or away.

While I was still feeling my way as a defensive lineman, I was making a name for myself on special teams. A lot of people didn't like to run full speed down the field and hit somebody.

But I did.

The vicious collisions that occur during kickoffs, however, are why these opening acts were known as the most dangerous play in football.

When people get to know me today, they say to me all the time, "Eric, you have such a big smile and are so nice to everybody. How did you play that mean game of football?"

"You should have seen me when I put my helmet on," I'll reply. "I was a totally different person. I talked junk and everything. I was the biggest trash-talker out there."

Like the time we were playing South Florida my freshman year. We were in the midst of our winning streak, and we had won the coin flip and elected to receive the opening kickoff. I lined up for my position, which happened to be right next to the South Florida bench.

Several USF players, helmets off, started woofin'. They were yapping things like:

"Hey, 52, you suck!"

"You think you're somethin'. You ain't nuthin'! You're garbage!"

"Get ready to get run over, 52!"

I thought about saying something back, but then the referee blew the whistle, and the South Florida kicker lofted the ball toward the goal line.

The runback was designed to come my way, so the lead block was on my shoulders. I was looking to blind-side somebody and take him out when, sure enough, the opportunity presented itself. One of the USF players wasn't looking where he should have been, and I knocked him on his butt. He tried to bounce off the ground, but I pushed him down again.

My stunning hit helped widen a running lane for our returner, Devin McCourty, who sprang free and churned up the sidelines. He returned the ball sixty yards before being knocked out-of-bounds. Now we had great field position.

Time to rub it in a little.

I ran up USF's sideline, dancing on my tippy toes.

"Woo-woo! Who's garbage now? Say something! You

saw what I just did to your boy! Say something to me now!"

Okay, I went crazy, but that's the emotional side of football. I'm glad that Coach Schiano didn't see me pulling that stunt, because he would have flipped out.

Finishing Strong

When the 2008 season was over, our 7-5 record made us bowl eligible. We were assigned to the Papa John's Pizza Bowl in Birmingham, Alabama. Our opponent would be the North Carolina State Wolfpack, a team that we had never played in our long football history at Rutgers.

I spent Christmas morning at home, where I opened my gifts—clothes and shoes—with Mom and Nicole. Then I had to check into the Hale Center at one p.m. for the team flight to Birmingham.

We came back from a 17-6 halftime deficit to mount a furious rally, and I had my hand in three stops that helped us come back in the fourth quarter to finish the 2008 season strong with a 29-23 victory over NC State.

The win made us 8-5—not too shabby for a team that was looking down the barrel of a 1-5 start. Our seven consecutive wins raised some eyebrows around the country.

I had gained ten pounds or so during the season, so now I was playing at 242. But that still wasn't enough weight be an impact player for something other than special teams.

Coach wanted me back in the weight room after a three-week break in early January. I was fine with that.

I had never shied away from hard work before, and I wasn't about to start now.

7

THE SCARLET WALK

ONE OF THE GREAT traditions at a tradition-rich school like Rutgers is the Scarlet Walk.

Two hours before every home game, our team would arrive at Rutgers Stadium in two buses after making the short drive from the Hyatt Regency in New Brunswick, where we spent the night in preparation.

After filing off the bus, we would march past a statue called the First Scarlet Knight—a life-size bronze statue of a nineteenth-century running back dressed in a woolen cap and carrying an overstuffed football. The monument commemorates the first college football game ever played back in 1869.

The entire Rutgers football team, dressed in our snazzy scarlet-red training outfits, would touch the First Scarlet Knight as we filed by. Then we'd follow a reddish-orange brick path to the locker room, where along the way cheerleaders shook their pom-poms and Rutgers fans of every age reached out to touch our hands.

Contributing to the festive atmosphere of school spirit would be the Rutgers University Marching Band—founded in 1915—playing one of our fight songs, "The Bells Must Ring" or "Colonel Rutgers." Hundreds, sometimes thousands, of red-clad Rutgers fans would politely clap, even cheer, as we passed by. The atmosphere was always electric. There's nothing like game day on a college campus.

I felt a sense of pride rise in my throat each time I made the pregame walk, and I always made sure to stop and give Mom a hug. You'd think my mother was the Official Team Mom from the way she exchanged high fives with so many of my teammates. They all knew her and enjoyed her infectious laugh and easy smile.

After I'd lined up at three spots during my freshman year—defensive end, defensive tackle, and fullback—

Coach Schiano settled on defensive tackle for my second season of college ball. Coming out of training camp, he had me and Charlie Noonan—a six-foot, two-inch, 295-pound defensive tackle from St. Joseph's Prep School in Philadelphia—rotating every four plays, meaning he would get the first four plays, then I'd get the next four. The platoon system worked for me.

My First Start

Thanks to a resurgence in the Rutgers football program, Rutgers Stadium was expanded during the off-season, adding around eight thousand seats and a large score-board in the south end zone. As we headed into my sophomore year, Coach Schiano preached about look-ing at every game as a "one-game season"—a concept that would keep us focused on the game at hand and not looking ahead to the next week. Unfortunately, we laid an egg against Cincinnati in our home opener, los-ing 47–15 before our largest home crowd ever, 53,737 people, and a nationwide audience looking in on ESPN.

I received my first career start in the fourth game of the 2009 season against the University of Maryland Ter-rapins. We had won two out of three games up to then, so this away game at Maryland would be a good measure of how good we would be. Mom and Nicole drove down from New Jersey to cheer me on, and I was keyed up when I ran out of the locker room as a starting player.

It was a drab, rainy day at Byrd Stadium, however, and our red cleats quickly got muddy on the Bermuda-grass field. We didn't let a little rain or mud stop us, however.

In the middle of the second quarter in a 10-10 game, the Terps' offensive guard and the center must have gotten their signals crossed, because they left the A gap wide open for me. When their quarterback, Chris Turner, went back to pass, I was in his kitchen before he even finished his seven-step drop. Turner saw me coming and huddled into a ball to absorb the hit he was going to receive. I bowled into him, wrapped my arms around his shoulders, and dumped him on the ground for a six-yard loss to record my first-ever sack.

Even though it was a first-down play on Maryland's own thirty-one-yard line in the second quarter, I felt like I had made a fourth-down goal-line stop to save a victory. I jumped up and began chopping my right forearm so rapidly that I could have felled one of those trees in the forest that Coach Schiano was always talking about. I was wild with excitement and could barely keep a lid on the joy bubbling to the surface.

A couple of my teammates immediately surrounded me with arms outstretched, telling me to cool it and deflecting attention from my chopping. In this case, no flag was thrown. I was lucky. Maybe the refs were looking the other way.

Next thing I knew, I was being replaced by Blair Bines and jogging back to the sidelines, where Coach Schiano was waiting for me.

He tore off his headset and got in my face. "Celebrate with your team!" he yelled. "Don't be an individual out there or you'll get a flag!"

He was right, of course. There was a line that I couldn't cross with the refs, and I had certainly bumped up right next to it, chopping and calling attention to myself. I was lucky there wasn't a yellow flag tossed high into the air for "excessive celebration," which would have cost us fifteen yards and an automatic first down in a tie game. Instead, we had the Terrapins pinned back on their twenty-four-yard line, second down and seventeen yards to go.

Advantage Rutgers. Sure enough, Turner tried to get it all back on the next play and threw into coverage, where our DB Devin McCourty intercepted the ball at midfield.

We played a good third quarter to take a 27–13 lead

going into the fourth. Maryland got the ball back with just under five minutes to go, but any dreams of coming back to tie us were snuffed when I sacked Turner for an eight-yard loss at the Maryland sixteen-yard line. This time I *did* celebrate with my team by exchanging the usual hand slaps and fist bumps. We won going away, 34-13.

I still keep a memento from that game. A sideline photographer took a great photo of me chopping away during that first-half sack. After my spinal cord injury, we had that photo blown up to a life-size cutout and mounted on my bedroom wall. Whenever I have visitors, I love telling the story behind the chop.

Special Teams Play

Our ninth game of the season was also on ESPN—a Thursday night matchup against twenty-third-ranked South Florida. Playing at home on national TV for the third time that fall was the charm. We killed the Bulls 31-0, and it felt great to be part of a defense that shut out a high-scoring team that had gotten on the scoreboard in every regular-season game in its thirteen-year history. Our impressive win made us bowl eligible for the fifth season in a row.

The St. Petersburg Bowl pitted the University of Central Florida Knights against the Rutgers Scarlet Knights, two 8-4 teams. This bowl game felt like a road game, however, because 20,000 UCF fans were among the crowd of 29,763 at Tropicana Field. We gave their fans something to cheer about on the opening kickoff when Quincy McDuffie of Central Florida ran past us for sixty-five yards all the way down to our thirty-one-yard line. I slapped my hands in frustration because I had a chance to make a tackle but I got blocked at the last second. Our kickoff team hung our heads a bit as we jogged toward the sideline to the sounds of their school band playing their fight song.

It looked like Central Florida had the momentum, but then linebacker Damaso Munoz made a big interception and we were back in business. We ended up kicking off a lot that game—eight times—as we ran over Central Florida, 45-24. Two of these kickoffs stand out in my mind.

In the first, I had a bead on the Knights' Quincy McDuffie and gave him a good lick. He bounced off the field and started talking trash. "Boy, you don't hit hard!" he yelled.

I wasn't going to stand for that. "I just knocked you

five yards from the place I hit you. Shut up and get off the field!"

The next time we kicked off, you can be sure I wanted his number, and this time, I hit him much harder. We exchanged more trash talk, but at the end of the night, we won our fourth bowl game in the last four years and gave our fans who made the trip to Florida a nice plane ride home.

A 9-4 season was quite an accomplishment, but the 2009 season could have been better. For decades, Rutgers fans would have thrown a parade for us down College Avenue after going 9-4, and we would have celebrated by eating fat sandwiches. But after five years of success, Rutgers fans were hungry for more.

So was everyone on the team. We all felt there was some unfinished business. We all knew something special would happen during my junior year.

Getting Wheels

As the sophomore season wrapped up, I was in the process of getting my first car. I had waited for my first ride for a *long* time. Ever since I got my license, I had really wanted a car of my own, but Mom didn't have the money.

I carefully saved up until I had five thousand dollars

resting in the bank, which I hoped was enough money to get the car I wanted: a 2002 Nissan Altima. Mom and I kept our eyes out on Craigslist and ads in the New Jersey *Star-Ledger*. We eventually found what I was looking for at a car dealer in Atlantic Highlands, which is in South Jersey.

Mom volunteered to drive down to the dealership and purchase the car so I wouldn't miss any classes. After taking a test drive and checking out the car, she signed the papers and drove the used Altima off the lot. She drove up to New Brunswick, and then we were going to drive back together to Atlantic Highlands to pick up her car.

On the way back to the car dealership, it started raining on Highway 35. We were about two miles from the car dealer when a young woman in the fast lane slammed on the brakes. Someone had cut her off, but her reaction was to come to a complete stop in the fast lane of a fast-moving highway.

There was nowhere for me to go. I slammed on my brakes, but I didn't stop in time. I slid right into her, crinkling her rear fender and doing a good number on my front bumper assembly. And then another car—a van— plowed into us, almost at full speed. Our air bags didn't deploy, but the back window exploded into shards of glass. Our crumpled sedan was pushed into the median, where it sustained more bumps and bruises. Glass was everywhere, even in our front seat. Thank goodness we weren't injured, but I sat there in total shock. The car that I had owned for a couple of hours—and invested my life savings in—was now a total wreck.

We had the car towed back to the dealership, and let's just say you should have seen the look on the salesman's face.

As soon as we received the insurance money, Mom and I started looking for a new used car. We soon found another 2002 Nissan Altima, but this one had fewer miles: just 67,000 miles. The dealer wanted around $8,500 for it, but we explained the situation and said that $5,000 was all I had. The car salesman "sharpened his pencil" and lowered the price to $6,000 *and* offered to throw in new tires and a tune-up. I was still $1,000 short, but Mom graciously agreed to cover the difference.

That was my mother, always digging deep for me.

"See, Mom? There was something about that other car," I said before I left for Rutgers. "I guess we weren't supposed to have that one. Look—now we found this new car, and we got a better deal. For a thousand dollars more, we got a car with thirty thousand fewer miles. They also gave us four new tires and a tune-up."

That's what I was always doing—looking at the bright side. Little did I know that in less than half a year, I would never drive that car again.

Everyone was telling me that I was a rising star in the Rutgers program, that my junior season would be my breakout year. I was ready. It had always been my dream as a little kid to go to the NFL and then retire and become a sports broadcaster, so if I was going to play football in the pros, I needed a big year.

I finally felt settled in at nose guard. I had played that one position all my sophomore year, and I knew what I had to do to become an impact player.

Coach Schiano still wanted me on special teams. In fact, he saw me as the catalyst of the kickoff team, the chairman of the board who set the tone. Now that I was going to be a junior, I could take even more of a leadership role.

I was also aware that NFL scouts look at *everything*— every play, including the kickoffs. Maybe they'd see some guy flying down the field, knocking blockers down right and left in a relentless pursuit of the kickoff returner.

Maybe they'd see a player who was fearless against a wedge of blockers, a player who always got his man.

Maybe they'd be like those Rutgers coaches who—during my freshman year of high school football—looked at game tape of another player and saw someone else making plays right and left. Maybe the NFL scouts would look at tape of my Rutgers games and say, "Who is that guy?"

I wanted them to find out who I was.

8

THE LEAD-UP TO GAME TIME

THE 2010 FOOTBALL SEASON would be Coach Greg Schiano's tenth at the helm of the Rutgers team, and while many Scarlet Knight fans appreciated how Coach had turned around a losing program that had once been a national laughingstock, a vocal minority wanted to see a Big East Conference championship year in and year out.

We didn't know what to expect for the 2010 season. Some preseason pundits were saying that we could be in a "rebuilding year" despite 8-5 and 9-4 seasons in 2008 and 2009, while others believed we could be a top-25 team and contend for the Big East championship.

Which way would the ball bounce?

I knew our defense would have to carry this team, but I thought our D was up to the task. We ranked right up there with the top programs during my sophomore year: We were No. 2 nationally in turnover margin, No. 4 in sacks, No. 15 against the run, No. 16 in scoring, and No. 18 in overall defense (out of 120 teams). Coach Schiano had us in an aggressive mind-set, and he liked to pull the trigger with blitzes. There was a great spirit on our side of the ball.

After I played nose guard throughout my sophomore year, Coach Schiano tweaked my position for the new season. He put me into a three-man rotation with Charlie Noonan, who also played nose guard, and my roommate, Scott Vallone, who played defensive tackle, meaning the three of us would rotate between nose guard and defensive tackle.

Under this new system, Charlie and Scott would start off and play four or five snaps, and then I would go in as a nose guard with Charlie coming off the field. After four or five plays, I would rotate over to Scott's position at defensive tackle and Charlie would come back in at nose

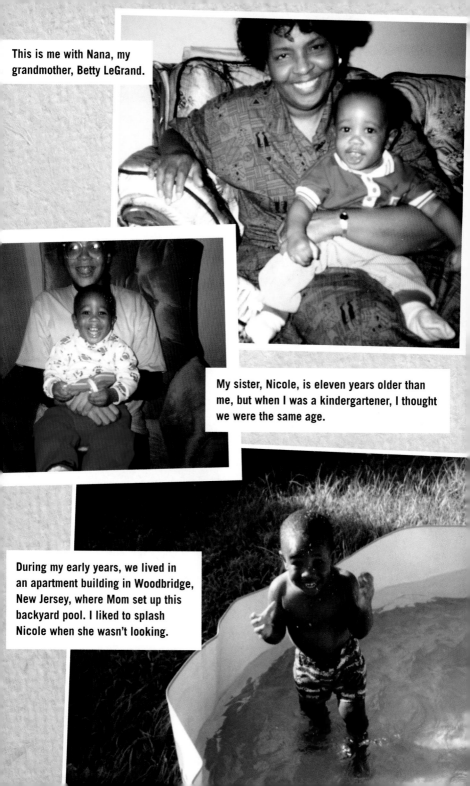

This is me with Nana, my grandmother, Betty LeGrand.

My sister, Nicole, is eleven years older than me, but when I was a kindergartener, I thought we were the same age.

During my early years, we lived in an apartment building in Woodbridge, New Jersey, where Mom set up this backyard pool. I liked to splash Nicole when she wasn't looking.

I loved riding my battery-operated "motorcycle" up and down the sidewalks in Woodbridge.

I was crazy about Batman. Here I'm getting ready to do some trick-or-treating on Halloween as the Caped Crusader.

Since I had so much energy, Mom thought it was a good idea to put me into Pop Warner football. I was six years old when this photo was taken—my last season of flag football.

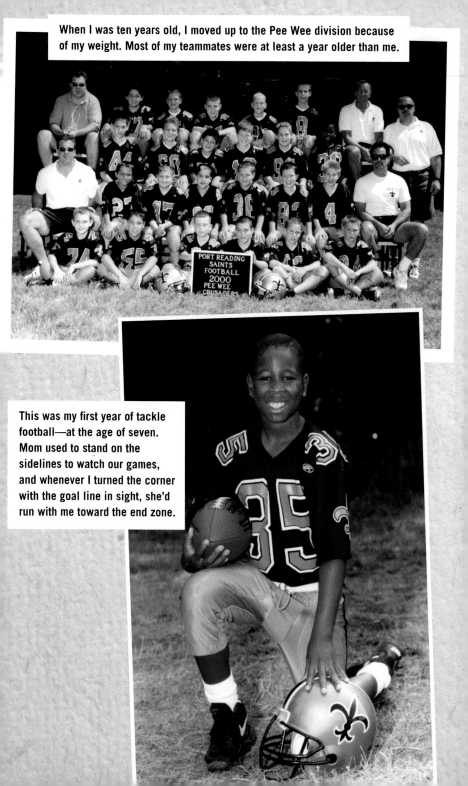

When I was ten years old, I moved up to the Pee Wee division because of my weight. Most of my teammates were at least a year older than me.

This was my first year of tackle football—at the age of seven. Mom used to stand on the sidelines to watch our games, and whenever I turned the corner with the goal line in sight, she'd run with me toward the end zone.

My most memorable childhood vacation was a Caribbean cruise with Mom, Nicole, Nana, and Auntie Cheryl. Everything was great except for the time they left me behind at the ship's camp for kids while they went onshore and had fun.

Even though I don't look too interested here, I actually loved playing baseball growing up and hitting my share of home runs in Little League.

WOODBRIDGE
LITTLE LEAGUE
2001
MAJOR
ORIOLES
33

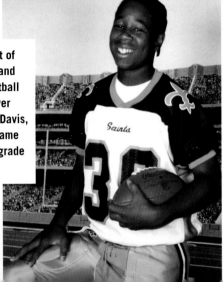

I wore No. 30 throughout most of my Pop Warner football days and while playing high school football at Colonia High because Denver Broncos running back Terrell Davis, my idol growing up, had the same number. I was in the seventh grade when this picture was taken.

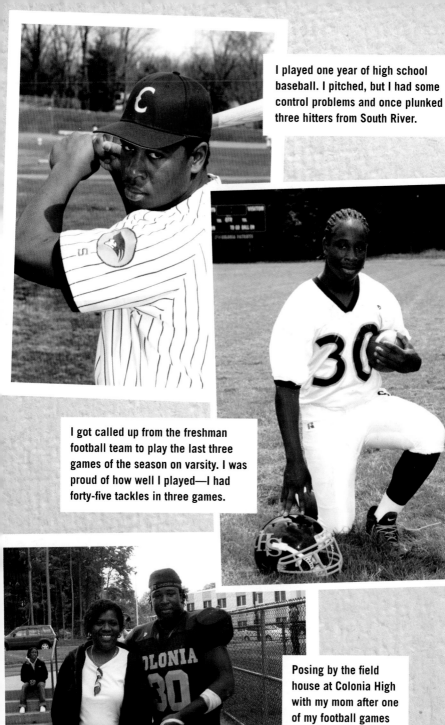

I played one year of high school baseball. I pitched, but I had some control problems and once plunked three hitters from South River.

I got called up from the freshman football team to play the last three games of the season on varsity. I was proud of how well I played—I had forty-five tackles in three games.

Posing by the field house at Colonia High with my mom after one of my football games senior year.

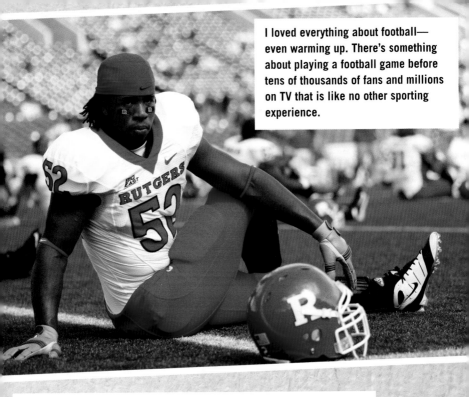

I loved everything about football—even warming up. There's something about playing a football game before tens of thousands of fans and millions on TV that is like no other sporting experience.

Here I make a textbook tackle—leading with my shoulder and wrapping up the runner to drive him to the ground. I had been coached to tackle correctly ever since my Pop Warner football days.

I was a special teams player at Rutgers—part of the kickoff and kickoff return teams. I loved sprinting down the field on a kickoff and making a big tackle inside the 20-yard line.

Football is a game of emotion, and you really do feel like you and your teammates are going into battle. Here I lift Steve Beauharnais after he made a great play.

My lovely girlfriend, Rheanne Sleiman, and I started dating five months before my injury in October 2010. Here we are in my room at the Kessler Institute for Rehabilitation in West Orange, New Jersey.

I have some great therapists at Kessler, and Sean McCarthy is one of my favorites. Here I'm hooked up to electrical stimulation devices a couple of months after my injury.

One week after my injury, the Rutgers football team played the University of Pittsburgh in Pittsburgh, where the Pitt fans showed their support for me.

PITT IS PULLING FOR ERIC LeGRAND

My Rutgers teammates have literally stood behind me—and have been so positive, telling me that one day I will leave my wheelchair.

I have a great team behind me, from Rheanne to my cousins Jazmin, Aaron, and James (left) and my Auntie Cheryl and Uncle Ariel (next to Mom). David Tyree, the Super Bowl hero who made the famous "helmet catch" in 2008, is directly behind me, along with other members of Team Believe who participated in a tough mudder obstacle course to raise money on my behalf.

Sharing my love for baseball with my nephews, Xavier and Isaac, at the Somerset Patriots minor league ballpark in Bridgewater, New Jersey.

Another great moment visiting with several New York Mets players at Citi Field. That's Jose Reyes (far left), who's now playing for the Miami Marlins, and several of my buddies: Ryan Don Diego, Brandon Hall, Drew Krupinski, and Evan Nadjavetsky.

When I stood with the assistance of this special metalized frame at Kessler in the summer of 2011, I tweeted out this picture along with a message: "Standing tall, we can't fall."

The Kessler Institute for Rehabilitation and the Christopher and Dana Reeve NeuroRecovery Network have teamed up to provide a great locomotor training program where I'm placed on a treadmill and held in place with a harness. Physical therapists hold me and move my legs as the treadmill "walks" me.

Mom is Caregiver No. 1, always on call, always there for me.

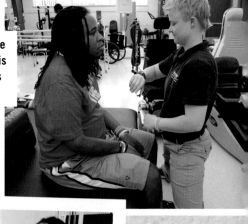

I can't believe how dedicated Buffy, one of my outpatient therapists at Kessler, is to my recovery. She continually pushes me, which is good.

These days I can't wait to get into my rehab at Kessler. Here is a technician putting on my walking shoes before I step into my special treadmill.

Here is my new team: the dedicated therapists at the Kessler Institute of Rehabilitation. Sitting next to me is Buffy, and in the row behind us (from the left) are Syndy, Roxanne, Lindsay, Prashad, and Jared.

Having a VW Routan—a handicap-accessible van—has greatly improved the quality of my life. I can go so many places with Mom, family, or friends behind the wheel. I can even get myself in and out of the van using my mouthpiece.

What an awesome guy. I got a chance to meet Tim Tebow at the end of the 2011 season at a home game in Denver, and he couldn't have been nicer—and his team had lost that day! Now he's playing in my backyard as a New York Jet.

Making the pilgrimage to Yankee Stadium in the Bronx, where I chatted with future Hall of Fame shortstop Derek Jeter, one of my favorite ballplayers growing up. That's my nephew Xavier hanging with us.

Nicole married Kenrick Harrigan a week before Christmas in 2011. I love having Kenny as a brother-in-law because he's always joking around and is so positive. He really fits in with our family.

I've received more than a dozen signed footballs wishing me the very best. Each and every football encourages me to keep believing that I will someday walk again.

The encouraging verse from the Bible (Philippians 4:13) says it all: "I can do all things through Christ who strengthens me."

That's me on the red carpet! I made my first trip to the West Coast in June 2012 when I received the first-ever Guysman Trophy for being the "manliest of men" at the Spike TV Guys Choice awards show. It was fun making my way down the red carpet with other sports and Hollywood celebrities.

BELIEVE 52

This picture says it all—and is just a fraction of the support I've received since my injury. Words will never be able to completely express my deep appreciation for the way people have reached out to me with love and support.

guard. We were three men sharing two positions. It was innovative, kept us physically fresh, and forced opposing offenses to make adjustments for us.

Coach Schiano also decided to shake things up with the way we practiced. Every football team I had ever played on always practiced in the afternoon. Rutgers was no different from every other major college football program. But Coach Schiano believed we were rushed throughout the day with our current afternoon practice schedule, and he was right. It did seem like we always had somewhere to go. His solution: practice early in the morning.

Real early. As in starting-at-six-a.m. early. At first, my teammates couldn't believe that Coach was doing this. College students weren't used to getting up at the crack of dawn. We were all night owls, and we all had friends who pulled all-nighters.

But six o'clock was when we had to check in at the Hale Center for breakfast. After we were finished eating, we'd head downstairs to the locker room, where we would dress for our seven fifteen team meeting. And then practice would follow the same schedule that we had for afternoons. We'd be off the field by eleven thirty or eleven forty-five.

When Coach shifted to a morning practice schedule, he showed that he liked to shake things up. He was always thinking proactively and outside the box. He also stressed the importance of giving back to the community. Coach Schiano asked each team member to volunteer his time for a worthy cause, such as visiting the sick or helping out with Habitat for Humanity, which builds homes for the disadvantaged.

I chose the Special Olympics as my cause during my sophomore year. During the summer leading into my junior season, I was among twenty-six Scarlet Knights who helped kick off the 2010 Special Olympics with the opening ceremonies at the College of New Jersey.

Coach Schiano served as the honorary coach for the Special Olympics and delivered an inspirational speech to open the games. Being part of the Special Olympics meant a lot to me, because I felt we were changing lives. The participants looked up to me as an athlete in my red number 52 jersey. Despite their physical limitations, they were willing to get out there and do their best. I loved their smiles, and from then on, I decided that I would always be a Special Olympics advocate and have been ever since.

Just one year later, Coach Schiano was unable to

make the opening ceremonies because of a family con-
flict. I filled in for Coach and led the opening ceremony
parade into the stadium, after which I addressed the athletes and their families from a stage lined with yellow
mums.

This time, though, I spoke from my wheelchair.

Early Birds

For my junior year, I lived off-campus with Devon Watkis
and Khaseem Greene, a linebacker from Elizabeth. We
leased a house where I had my own bedroom and a nice
queen-size bed. Oh, and I should mention my first flat-
screen TV, which Mom and Nicole got for me as an early
birthday present. Getting our own place was a good way
to teach me to manage my money, because I had to help
with keeping the bills paid.

Even though there were changes in my life—practice
times, my responsibilities on defense—one thing was
constant for me with Rutgers football: my role on special teams. I heard Coach Schiano tell his assistants that
my abilities on kickoffs and kickoff returns were assets
that he didn't want to take away from the team. I was
our main man, the guy running down the field crack-
ing heads and making a statement. I had always loved

special teams and the camaraderie among us. There's no other place I wanted to be when we were kicking off or receiving. Special teams were my forte.

We started off the season with a soft touch on the schedule, Norfolk State, a Division I-AA school where the players are smaller and, presumably, not as talented. We played at home on a Thursday night before a big crowd, but we didn't give our fans much to cheer about. Our offense couldn't get untracked, and we were only leading 6-0 at the half.

We eventually put Norfolk State away, 31-0, but it wasn't pretty. I played well on special teams and didn't allow the Spartans any big runbacks on a half dozen kick-off returns, but I didn't play much on defense. I thought we were going to implement the new rotation, but the defensive coaches barely called my name.

The same thing happened against a lightly regarded Division I school, Florida International. We squeaked out a 19-14 win, but our offense continued to misfire. Although we won and had a 2-0 record, I was kind of down afterward, since I didn't get to contribute much on defense. Some rotation plan.

Two days later, Coach Schiano called me up to his office. At first, I wondered what I had done wrong, but

Coach quickly put me at ease. "I was breaking down the film, and I realized that you've barely played this year. We're going to fix that," he said. He explained that our new defensive line coach didn't understand the rotation system that he had installed into the game plan for Charlie, Scott, and me.

"Don't worry," Coach said. "You're going to be seeing a lot of action from here on out. We need you out there."

It was great to hear Coach express confidence in me, because I'd been thinking about going in and asking him what was going on. Now I could turn my full attention to our next opponent, North Carolina. The feeling on the Rutgers team was that this game against the Tar Heels would reveal how good we really were.

Our offense, led by quarterback Tom Savage, sputtered against UNC. We couldn't run the ball, and our passing game couldn't get untracked. Even though we led 10-7 at the half, we should have been ahead by two touchdowns. Time and again, the defense came up with big stops, producing turnovers to keep things close. I played a lot of snaps this time around.

We fell behind 17-13, but we were knocking on the door at the six-yard line midway through the fourth quarter. Then disaster struck when Tom was intercepted on a poorly thrown pass on the seven-yard line. I rushed onto the field with the defense, and we held North Carolina to a three-and-out. A short punt had us back in business on the Tar Heels' thirty-four-yard line—great field position—but three incompletes and a sack meant we had to swallow a tough loss.

There was a lot of frustration in the locker room afterward, because we had been pointing toward this game since training camp started. It was like someone had ripped the hearts out of our chests. We wanted to get back at them for whupping us on our home field my freshman year. But the plain truth was that we made too many mistakes, and they capitalized on them.

Then it was the same thing all over again the following week: We lost our homecoming game to Tulane by a nearly identical score, 17-14. Once again we couldn't run and couldn't complete enough passes. Savage was injured and replaced by true freshman quarterback Chas Dodd, who performed well but threw a pick on our last drive of the game. The aggravation worsened when our kickoff return team sprang Joe Lefeged for a ninety-five-yard return for a touchdown, but the scoring play was nullified by a holding penalty.

I'll admit the Scarlet Knights were reeling after that

pair of defeats. We could have been undefeated, but *coulda* and *shoulda* don't count for much in football. We had to regroup quickly, because we were playing the University of Connecticut on a Friday night on ESPN—and a national TV audience would be looking in.

I always liked playing on weeknights, since that meant our game would be nationally televised. Our great fans were always more crazy at night games, too. For the UConn game, they organized a "blackout," which meant they would all arrive at Rutgers Stadium dressed in black T-shirts. There was something very intimidating about the wall of black the fans created in the stands. I knew our student section—some holding cardboard axes they used to "chop" after a big play—would be really fired up.

We got things going our way in the first quarter with a quick stop on defense, which put the football into the hands of Chas Dodd, who was still subbing for the injured Tom Savage. Chas wasn't afraid to take shots down the field; he was an aggressive playmaker who could make things happen. He was a competitor.

On the first set of downs, Chas dropped back and flung a forty-six-yard touchdown pass to give us a 7-0 lead—a good start for an offense that didn't have many long bombs or long runs up to this point. Now we were kicking off. San San Te's kick sailed toward the left—my side of the field.

I sprinted toward the end zone, but I had a double team coming at me. My job was to either split the double team, which means go through it, or stay to the outside. Instead, I tried something fancy and moved inside, but the two blockers pushed me all the way inside, which opened up a huge hole. Next thing I knew, I heard their fans going crazy as UConn's Nick Williams cut back through the hole and ran untouched on a hundred-yard touchdown sprint. Just like that, it was 7-7, and our early lead was history.

I was fuming. A year earlier, UConn had had another hundred-yard run for a touchdown against us, and now this.

"Receiving team!" bellowed our special teams coach, Robb Smith.

I was back on the field with the kickoff receiving team. I think everyone felt a bit ticked by UConn's coast-to-coast touchdown run. This time it was our turn to create a running lane for Joe Lefeged. I had a key block that sprung him loose, and Joe nearly went all the way. He was chased down on UConn's fourteen-yard line after dashing for seventy-five yards, and I remember running after him, screaming in delight after taking it back on UConn.

Rutgers versus UConn turned out to be one of those lead-changing contests between two well-matched teams. We found ourselves down a touchdown with less than four minutes to go. Crunch time. Our young quarterback, Chas Dodd, stepped up and threw a fifty-two-yard touchdown pass to tie the game 24–24, and then he connected on a forty-five-yard pass to set up the game-winning field goal. San San Te popped the ball through the uprights from thirty-four yards to give us our first lead with just thirteen seconds left to play, and moments later we ran off the field with helmets high, celebrating a 27–24 victory.

An epic home win like that made me feel a lot better, but I knew we couldn't let mistakes on special teams happen again—not if we were going to make this a standout season.

Army Rations

Coach Schiano was tough on me during the week of practice leading up to our next game, against Army.

But it wasn't because of the long touchdown run by UConn following our kickoff. Every year, Coach changed the defense whenever we played one of the service academies, Army or Navy. This time around, I was struggling with my footwork, because it was different from our normal defense.

Coach wanted me to take a certain pivot step with my left or right foot, depending on which side of the center I was on. It's rather complicated to describe, but Coach instructed me to "read and react" to the direction the guard in front of me was going. If their offensive guard went "out"—meaning he left his place on the line to block someone else—I had to resist the urge to follow him with my eyes but instead keep my vision focused on the gap he had just vacated. If the guard went "in," meaning he stayed put and tried to block me, I had to ride him and win the position battle. If he veered up a little bit to take me in a different direction, then I would have to push him off and watch for the center coming back at me.

All these variations would happen in a half second, literally a blink of an eye. From this initial half-second read, I had to know exactly where to go. I wasn't finding this part of the game easy. It was natural for my eyes to follow the guard, because he was my man. But sometimes the guard was a decoy and his job was to block me or keep me confused on where the play was going.

I studied these moves on film and thought I had them down, but in practice I had problems with my reads and pivoting my feet. Each time I made a mistake, Coach Schiano was all over me. He wasn't upset, but he wasn't letting anything slide.

Thankfully, I was in much better shape by Thursday's practice. I had watched enough film by then to know what to look for, so my pivot steps were improving a lot. I knew I'd be ready to play on Saturday afternoon.

Our game against Army was a continuation of a series that began in 1891, and this would be the thirty-seventh time the two teams had met. Talk about evenly matched: Our series was tied, 18-18. Even though this would be a home game for us, we wouldn't be playing at Rutgers Stadium. Instead the game was set for New Meadowlands Stadium in East Rutherford, New Jersey. The rationale behind playing at New Meadowlands—about an hour-long drive from Piscataway—was purely financial. The New Meadowlands Stadium Corporation offered Rutgers $2.7 million to bring the game to the new stadium, money that would help fund other sports programs at Rutgers—like my girlfriend Rheanne's soccer team.

The reason the word "New" was in front of

"Meadowlands" was because the stadium had just opened a few months earlier. Built at a cost of $1.6 billion, New Meadowlands Stadium was the home of the New York Jets and New York Giants and replaced the aging Giants Stadium located on the same site. The new stadium seated 82,566 and came with all the bells and whistles. There were twenty giant high-def LED pylons at the north and east entrances that displayed videos of the players from both teams.

The Rutgers team stayed at the Hyatt Regency in New Brunswick, as per our custom every night before a home game. I usually roomed with Scott Vallone, but Coach Schiano wanted me to stay with Michael Larrow, a six-foot, three-inch, 258-pound defensive end who was a true freshman. The coaching staff asked me to mentor Michael, help him get mentally prepared for the game. He was still feeling his way with big-time Division 1 football.

Actually, I was a bit upset that my routine was thrown off. Not that I didn't want to help Michael, but Scott and I had been football-game roommates for a couple of seasons, and that was the pregame routine I was used to.

Breakfast was served until eight thirty, so we were allowed to sleep in until eight a.m., which—after nearly two months of morning practice—felt like a luxury. I liked to keep breakfast light because there was always a pregame meal, so I had a toasted bagel with butter and a bowl of my favorite cereal, Kellogg's Frosted Flakes. That would last me until our pregame meal at ten fifteen a.m. Game time was set for two p.m.

There were the usual pregame nerves that morning—a mixture of excitement coupled with a focused attitude. We were going to war with a team that wanted to do the same thing we were trying to do: win a game.

After our defensive team meeting, we had a fifteen-minute break before our pregame meal, so I went back to my room and opened my playbook to review our defensive formations and blitzes. I put on my headphones and listened to Lil Wayne on my iPod—I liked how hip-hop music pumped me up before big games, and Lil Wayne was one of my favorites.

A few minutes before ten fifteen a.m., I went downstairs for our pregame meal. We were a little less than four hours before the opening kickoff—a time when you zone in. No more joking around or laughing. Cell phones turned off. Time to get locked and loaded.

I ate what I always did right before a game: lasagna, a piece of bread, and white rice. Carbo loading. When I finished my last bite, I returned to my room to collect my belongings. Then we had a five-minute team meeting at 10:50, during which Coach Schiano gave us a motivational talk. As usual, he was really fired up.

"These guys aren't your friends!" Coach bellowed. "They are out there to win a game just like you, and they are trained to go to war! So you better be ready at all times for anything, because they will do anything to win!"

Got it, Coach.

After Coach Schiano was finished inspiring the troops, we boarded the team buses at eleven a.m. for the drive to New Meadowlands Stadium.

As the buses pulled up to Giants Stadium—that's what I still called the stadium, showing that old habits die hard—I saw all the amazing LED screens affixed to surfaces above the players' entrance. The brilliant jumbo screens were the size of billboards and switched from one digital picture to another. I saw my teammate Antonio Lowery up there about twenty feet tall. He was one of our linebackers, one of our good players, but he was getting the star treatment. *Wow, this is serious,* I thought. *We're going to be playing in Giants Stadium.*

I was excited for another reason: Practically all my family was going to be there to watch me play. Normally players get only four complimentary seats, but when you added up the family and friends, I needed about twenty tickets. I got extra seats from out-of-state teammates who weren't using their allotment.

On the family side, Mom was there; my sister, Nicole, her fiancé, Kenrick Harrigan, and their son, Xavier; Auntie Cheryl and her husband, Uncle Ariel, plus their three kids: Jazmin, Aaron, and James; and my father, Donald McCloud, which I appreciated. I didn't see him much, but he was cordial with Mom, so he arrived with his brother, my uncle Ricky, and my cousin Jackie Bonafide.

I had old friends from the neighborhood in my "box," too. My old Pop Warner coach, Jack Nevins, came with his wife, Sue—the first time she would ever see me play at Rutgers—and their son John. The Liquori family sat in Mom's section, too. I was practically raised on the heavenly pizza from Rocco's Pizzeria, spun from the hands of Rocco Liquori. I grew up playing baseball with his son Alex.

Because of all the friends and family members, Mom went the extra step and hosted a tailgate party in the stadium parking lot before the game. Normally, she hopscotched other tailgate parties when we played at home, where she hung out with Scott Vallone's parents or Devon

Watkins's parents. But this time Uncle Ricky insisted on doing our own tailgate. Some folks brought the hot dogs and hamburgers, others brought the chips and dip, and some brought the beer and soda pop. They did things up right at Mom's tailgate.

Mom left the tailgate early to watch us warm up inside the stadium. Scott Vallone and I usually came out on the field around ninety minutes before kickoff in our "lowers"—pants and cleats. That was one of our traditions we did every game to stretch and limber up. Mom came down to the first row behind the Rutgers bench and tried to make eye contact with me. We had a little tradition worked out before every game: When our eyes met, she'd point at me, and I would nod my head.

I knew Mom would be out there, so I allowed my eyes to scan the nearly empty seats behind the Rutgers bench. That's when I saw Mom's happy face. When she noticed me looking in her direction, she waved her hand.

I nodded to her, and then I went about my business. I was already locked into the game.

An Early Lead

Even though our energy level was high, Army drew first blood, with the Black Knights dominating the first half to take a 17-3 lead into the locker room. We had only ourselves to blame: a blocked punt by Army—a special teams play—and a recovery at our twelve-yard line led to their first touchdown. Chas Dodd wasn't getting the protection he needed, and we were making too many mistakes and getting hit with too many penalties.

There were some frustrated Scarlet Knights in the locker room at intermission, and Coach Schiano wasn't in a gracious mood. He ripped into us about what we were doing wrong—missed assignments, lazy tackling, and ill-timed penalties. "There's a whole half left, so we can't worry about the fourth quarter now. We have to chop to each individual play one by one," he said.

We kicked off to start the second half. Even though San San Te's kick was short, we held Army's return man Joshua Jackson to a seventeen-yard runback. Then the Black Knights ran their triple-option offense to perfection—three, four yards a pop—and advanced to our twenty-four-yard line, with a third-and-four.

Army had rushed the ball down our throats *eleven* straight times, so you might say that I was expecting the run. Trent Steelman handed the ball off to Jared Hassin, and I was in the pile that stopped him for a one-yard gain.

Fourth-and-three from the twenty-three-yard line. Army was just outside their red zone. I expected the Black Knights to kick a field goal and take the three points, but their coach, Rich Ellerson, waved his offense back onto the field. They were going for it. Perhaps Ellerson sensed that if Army made a first down, they'd work their way to the end zone. That would put us in a huge 24-3 hole, which would be a big task for our young offense.

Then Steelman dropped back to pass. Our linebackers and corners were ready, and his pass fell incomplete.

That was the break we needed. Our offense mounted a *twenty-one*-play drive that took up the rest of the third quarter. (We had several false starts that extended the drive.) I had never had such a long break in my life, sitting on the bench and resting up for the next series of downs.

I stood up, though, when Coach Schiano rolled his own set of dice on fourth down. It was fourth-and-two on Army's three-yard line, so technically we could still get a first down, but there was no doubt that Coach was going for six points.

Chas rolled to his right and hit Kordell Young in the end zone, and with the extra point, it was a one-score game, 17-10. All the momentum was on our side, and when our well-rested defense got a quick stop, the Scarlet Knights scored the tying touchdown with 5:16 to go on another Chas Dodd touchdown pass, this time to Mark Harrison.

"Kickoff team!" yelled Robb Smith, our special teams coach.

I jogged out on the field, reviewing the instructions my coaches had given me in the pregame meetings. The Army players were very precise and very tough on kickoff returns, which meant I could expect to be double-teamed. They were also aware from game film that I was one of the guys to watch out for.

"Go around to the outside and get right back in your lane," Coach Smith told me. With his advice ringing in my ears, I knew exactly what to do to avoid the double team. A tackle inside the twenty-yard line would pin Army back deep in their own territory.

The time was 4:46 p.m., Eastern Standard Time, on October 16, 2010—a moment that will forever be etched in my mind.

9

THE COLLISION

Up in the broadcast booth, Bob Picozzi was calling the play-by-play for ESPN3, which streamed the game live on the internet on pay-per-view.

"It's late in the fourth quarter. Tie game. So we have a new football game with 5:16 left."

I knew the Army receiving unit would have two guys waiting for me. They had been throwing a double team at me on every kickoff, and this was the fourth of the afternoon.

"San San Te to kick off. This is a good one."

This time, the Black Knights had Malcolm Brown, a talented and fast slotback, back deep. Their regular returner, Joshua Jackson, hadn't had a good day against us, so maybe Brown would give them a spark.

I was in a full sprint as San San Te's kickoff settled into the arms of the Army kick returner a few yards inside the goal line. He was on my side of the field. In fact, if you drew a straight line between us, I had a direct beeline on him. There were thirty-five yards between us, but we were each running at full speed, so the distance was closing fast.

"Inside the five. It's Malcolm Brown . . ."

I was getting excited because the play was coming straight at me. I knew where I wanted to hit him. I was going to throw my shoulder right into his chest. As the distance closed between us, I remembered to set up my body.

His lead blockers were starting to pick up our people as the gap between us narrowed. Just as I expected, two guys tried to slow me down, but I made a quick juking move and slipped past them. In a split second, I saw Brown right in front of me. I had a clear shot.

Instinct took over. Just before I exploded into him, one of my teammates dove for his legs. Brown responded by swiveling his hips and twisting ever so slightly as he reached the impact zone.

I was set to throw my shoulder into his midsection—the classic "bite the ball" way to tackle—but Brown had been spun a bit. Instead of hitting him in the chest with my shoulder—where I was aiming—my helmet rammed into the back of his left shoulder, striking his collarbone. The collision between helmet and bone made a sickening sound that ricocheted through the stadium. It all happened in tenths of a second.

"Oooh! What a great open-field hit by Eric LeGrand, who was shaken up by the play...."

When I nailed him, my body instantly went stiff, and I felt like I was in a movie. My vision immediately blurred, and everything slowed down. I fell to the ground like a giant oak that had been cut down, landing on my back.

If you watch the replay on YouTube—which I have numerous times—the crowd makes an immediate *oooh* after we collided. That's how loud the sound of impact was. If my head had been just a few more degrees upright, I would have gotten up, dusted myself off, and gone about my business. But as it happened, the colossal impact between the tip of my helmet and the thin padding covering Malcolm's collarbone resulted in my spinal cord taking the full force of the crushing blow.

The last thing I felt were my legs going down to the ground. My body went *ding*, and a loud ringing sound swirled through my brain.

I knew something bad had happened. Really bad. Just how horrible, I didn't know, but this was way beyond any hits I had received or dished out on the football field.

Once I hit the ground, though, a rush of adrenaline surged through my body. *You gotta get up! Get up!* I had always pushed myself to my knees and gotten up after being knocked down—ever since I was a first grader, when Charlie Schwartz sent me flying into telephone poles next to the basketball hoop.

This time, however, I couldn't move anything—my legs, my arms, or my torso. I tried pulling myself off the ground again, but nothing happened. I could move my head slightly, but that was about it.

Must be a legit full stinger, I thought. A stinger is a neurological injury that athletes in high-contact sports like football, rugby, or ice hockey sometimes experience. A nerve in the spine or neck gets pinched from contact, and the result is a "stinging" sensation in the affected area. But I couldn't feel any part of my body stinging, so it couldn't be that.

Two teammates, defensive backs Duron Harmon and Patrick Kivlehan, came over to see how I was doing—but they immediately stepped back. A couple of other teammates also determined that something didn't look right. They looked over to our sideline and made a waving motion, but our trainers were already on the run. Coach Schiano was fast on their heels.

I looked out through my mask and kept still. I quickly realized I was out of breath and needed air. I gasped and tried to say the words *I can't breathe* to anyone who could hear me, but I couldn't press out the air necessary to form the words in my larynx.

Two Rutgers trainers, a bit winded from the long sprint, came into my vision and knelt beside me.

"Is it your head or your neck?" asked one in a frantic voice.

I can't breathe!

At least, that's what I wanted to say, but the words wouldn't come out. I tried to mouth the thought, but with my helmet still on, my trainers couldn't read my lips.

"Can you feel me touching your hand?" asked the other trainer.

I didn't answer. I couldn't move. I couldn't breathe.

"Head or neck?" yelled the first trainer, the panic rising in his voice.

Once again, I couldn't form the words.

"Head or neck, Eric?" he repeated.

My eyes bulged in fear. I was panicking myself. I thought I was going to run out of air any second and die. They had to do something to help me!

I tried to mouth the words *I can't breathe, I can't breathe*, but I wasn't having any success.

Coach Schiano leaned into my view. He was on his knees with a furrowed brow. Coach looked as concerned as I had ever seen him. When he had sprinted across the field, he shot a quick prayer heavenward: *Please, Lord, just let him be knocked out.*

"Eric, you just got to pray," he said to me. "Just pray that you're going to be fine."

I can't breathe, Coach. I can't breathe. This time I rasped some of the sounds, but neither Coach nor anyone else could understand what I was trying to get across. What I didn't know at the time was that when I severely injured my spinal cord, there was an immediate loss of nerve supply to the entire body, including my heart and blood vessels. A sudden and profound drop in blood pressure occurred, which is known as "spinal shock."

I sensed urgency from the next wave of responders who surrounded me, but I also heard the voices of other players:

He's probably got a concussion. He'll be fine.

No, I saw him fall. I don't like the way he hit the ground.

I hope he'll be okay.

It's bad, man.

In the stadium, a quiet murmur fell over the crowd. Mom was sitting in a lower field level section on the twenty-five-yard line with a direct view of the collision. She was becoming more panicked by the second. Mom stood next to my sister, Nicole, who was next to her fiancé, Kenny. On Mom's right side was Sue Nevins. Everyone close to me was there to cheer me on to victory. Now they all looked on in horror as I lay motionless on the field.

"Don't worry," said Mrs. Nevins, trying to be helpful. "He's going to be okay."

Something about the way I fell didn't sit right with Mom. She had seen me get knocked on my butt hundreds of times—but never like this. Every time in every other game, I had immediately risen to my feet. But there was something grotesquely different in what she had just witnessed, and it was the way I fell to the ground and bounced on the turf like I was a teeter-totter. My legs, which were raised off the ground, had gone stiff as a board.

Her heart was in her throat as she watched Coach Schiano, trainers, and medical staff form a circle around me. A white cart marked EMS zoomed across the field. It was at that moment that the situation went from *Oh my God what happened?* to *This could be really serious.*

Everyone was mute around her, mirroring the hushed silence inside the cavernous stadium. Mom scanned the field, trying to process information. Every player on the Rutgers and Army teams had taken a knee. Some bowed their heads in prayer and didn't care who knew. Others had pensive looks of disbelief at what was happening. All were grim-faced and silent. Tears began forming in Mom's eyes. She knew something really, really bad had happened to me.

Mom suddenly saw a distressed man in a Rutgers Windbreaker running in her direction, waving for her to come on the field. He was part of Coach Schiano's security detail, and Coach had told him to make sure that he got my mom.

"Ms. LeGrand? Can you come with me?"

My mother didn't hesitate to gather her purse and light jacket. She had to be with her baby.

"You want to come?" she asked Nicole.

"I'm coming," my sister responded.

Mom held Nicole close and prayed that I would be okay. She wore a scarlet-red Rutgers jersey over a T-shirt, emblazoned with number 52 on the front and back. Across the back of my mother's shoulders were these two words:

LeGRAND'S MOM

What Was Going On?

Sometimes people who have been put in incredibly stressful situations—such as major trauma—will say they felt a sense of peace during the moment of the injury. They'll describe how everything slowed down, allowing them time to grasp their new reality with greater clarity.

But I wasn't feeling any sense of peace. I was in a fight for my life. I feared the worst, that this might be my time to leave this earth, and I fought to hold on to the next minute, the next breath.

I heard Coach Schiano's voice. "Slow down," he said. "Slow everything down. You're going to be fine, but just keep on praying."

I didn't pray, not right then. I was too busy trying to breathe. A few moments later, however, I did think to ask: *God, what is going on?*

It seemed like a logical question. Even though I hadn't gone to church much growing up, I certainly believed in God and his son, Jesus Christ. This seemed like one of those foxhole moments to ask a question like that, but I didn't get an answer. So I prayed some more. My mind pleaded with the Almighty that I would be all right.

God, please let me catch my breath.

God, please let me get up.

God, please let me move.

God, what is going on?

Six or seven emergency personnel took a few moments to gingerly lift me atop the backboard and securely fasten me.

Once the responders were satisfied that I was stable and immobilized—which included taping my helmeted head to the backboard—eight or nine men lifted me up and placed me on the bed of the EMS cart. The act of lifting me off the ground gave me a gasp of much-needed air.

As the driver swung the cart around to take me off the field, I heard the public address announcer say, "Eric LeGrand."

Thousands of fans clapped respectfully. Because of the subdued, polite applause, I desperately wanted to give the crowd a thumbs-up from my prone position on the cart—to let them know I would be all right. That should be simple enough—raising my hand with thumb extended into the air.

But I couldn't move any of my fingers. It felt like there were a thousand pounds holding my thumb down. As I lay on the backboard, I wanted to look at my right hand, thinking that if I could somehow see my fingers, then my hand would move the thumb on my command. But I was immobilized, and my entire right arm remained limp.

This is so weird. Maybe my body was in shock—and that's why I couldn't move a muscle. I kept trying and trying, but nothing worked. I had shaken off so many injuries in the past, but this was something I had never experienced before.

The EMT cart pulled into the tunnel, shielded from public view. Team officials escorted Mom and Nicole to my side.

When I saw my mother, she looked scared. I summoned the strength to say, "I'm going to be okay, Mom," but I garbled the words and my voice was barely above a whisper.

I was rolled into an ambulance, and the EMTs directed Mom to get into the front seat. Nicole would follow us in her car. I remembered something. "Mom," I whispered.

My mother leaned closer from her passenger seat.

"Call Rheanne," I said. I wanted Mom to reach my girlfriend and let her know that I would be all right. She was back in New Brunswick, watching the game on her computer since it was on ESPN3.

A paramedic placed an oxygen mask over my mouth and nose. I was surprised that the mask didn't help as much as I thought it would. I would have loved a lot more air filling my lungs, but then I blacked out before we left the stadium.

I remember being aware of arriving at the hospital in an enclosed garagelike building, although everything was blurry. I heard all sorts of echoes as I was unloaded from the van and quickly wheeled through open doors. Awaiting me was Mom with Nicole. I was taken to some type of emergency room, where I heard a sound of *boom-boom, boom-boom.* I had no idea what it was. The

151

lights were bright as people fluttered about me, moving quickly.

From that point until basically the following Wednesday, I barely remember anything at all, but Mom has since filled me in on all the activity and commotion that happened while I was in and out of a deep semi-coma.

I had been taken to the Hackensack University Medical Center in Hackensack, New Jersey, five miles away from the Meadowlands. Around forty-five minutes after my arrival, Dr. Roy Vingan walked into the waiting room, where Mom, tons of family members, teammates like Scott Vallone and his family, and old friends from Avenel like Nate Brown and Brandon Hall had gathered. The neurosurgeon pulled my mother aside with a touch of her elbow.

"Eric cannot move," he said. "He has broken his neck and needs surgery." He further explained that the collision had cracked two vertebrae near the top of my spinal column—the C3 and the C4. "Right now, he cannot move his arms or legs."

Mom was in a daze. She didn't know what to say.

"Will he . . . will he be all right?" my mom managed.

"We don't know," the doctor replied. "We will be attempting to repair what we can during surgery. And then we have to wait and see. Seventy-two hours is key.

Before we start, you can go see him."

My mom's eyes brightened. I'm told that I was awake, but I don't remember seeing Mom before I went into surgery.

"You're going to be okay," she whispered. "You're going to be okay. The doctors say you have to have surgery, so be brave. I'm here for you. I love you."

My eyes were open, and Mom says I looked at her, but I didn't know who she was. In fact, I had no idea what was happening.

My operation began around eight on Saturday evening. For the next nine hours, a group of doctors performed delicate surgery to stabilize my spine. The reason the operation took so long is that they had to align my broken neck in such a way that I would be able to breathe and swallow in the future. What many people don't realize is that if a broken neck heals in a zigzag fashion, the patient will have difficulty breathing and swallowing the rest of his or her life.

Coach had presided over a somber postgame press conference, even though we had beaten Army 23-20 in overtime. Gripping the podium tightly and biting his lip, he leaned forward and made an opening statement to the assembled reporters and news cameras.

The pain clearly registered on his face. He answered several football questions and then excused himself, saying he wanted to get over to the hospital.

Little did Coach Schiano know the win over Army would be our last victory of the 2010 season. Rutgers would go on to lose six consecutive games, unable to overcome a black cloud that had settled over the program when Malcolm Brown and 1 crashed into each other like runaway freight trains.

Coming Out of Surgery

At five in the morning, when it was still pitch-dark outside, Dr. Vingan startled the dazed crowd in the waiting room with his entrance. Sleeping bodies stirred in the waiting room. Once again, he pulled my mother aside.

"I'm sorry for taking so long," he began as if he needed to apologize. "We never expected the surgery to take as long as it did. First of all, Eric is stable. The reason everything took so long is because we operated on the front of his neck, and then we had to flip him over to do some things in the back of his neck. We were not happy with the initial results, so we had to redo some things. It's important that his spinal column line up."

Dr. Vingan took his time to explain that the spinal cord does not have to be severed to cause paralysis. The spinal cord carries electrical impulses from the brain through a jellylike tube of neural tissues out to my arms and legs and back again. Protecting this soft tube of neural tissues is a spinal column made up of thirty-three bones, or vertebrae. The vertebrae at the topmost portion of the spine are numbered one through eight. The higher the injury on the spinal column, the closer the injury is to the brain. The closer to the brain, the more likely the injury will affect your ability to move your arms and legs and have feeling.

"Eric's injury happened to the C3 and C4 vertebrae, which is quite high," Dr. Vingan said. "We estimate that Eric has a zero to five percent chance of regaining neurological function."

"That low?" Mom didn't like hearing that.

"I'm afraid so, Ms. LeGrand."

She decided that she didn't want any doctors talking to me. She didn't want me to know what the medical experts thought about my chances. She wanted me to stay positive. She hadn't given up hope. Mom believed in me, and she would help me fight through this.

On Sunday evening, Mom and Rheanne were in the

intensive care unit. In my semiconscious state, I sensed I had visitors.

And then I remembered something—*practice*. I had to get to practice.

"I gotta go," I whispered. "Coach doesn't like it if we're late to practice."

Keep in mind that I was flat on my back, barely able to utter these words because of all the tubes down my throat.

"It's okay, Eric," Rheanne soothed, fighting back tears. "You don't have to go to practice today."

"Did you win today?"

For some reason, I had correctly remembered that the women's soccer team had a game on Sunday afternoon.

"No, we tied St. John's, but I played well." What Rheanne didn't say was that her coach took her out after the first half because he could see that she was clearly not herself. She didn't include that information because she didn't want me to worry about her.

Later that evening, several close friends were allowed to see me: Tyler Jackow, Brandon Hall, and Joey LaSala. Once again, I mouthed a question that was barely above a whisper: "Hey, guys, what are we doing tonight?"

"E, I think you just need to chill for the night," Tyler said.

I must have repeated the question three times. We continued trying to have a conversation, but one by one, the guys would excuse themselves to step outside my ICU room. And that's where they'd break down and sob out of my earshot.

I had no idea that people were crying after seeing me. Every time somebody came into my room, it was all positive energy:

It's going to be all right, Eric.

Everything is going to be fine.

You'll be playing football in no time.

But the kicker of that Sunday evening was when Coach Schiano stepped into my room. He expressed love and concern for me, but I interrupted him with a random question that I couldn't get out of my mind. "Coach, there's one thing I always wanted to ask you. Do you think I can play in the NFL?"

Coach Schiano never blinked an eye. "Your chances are as good as anyone else's," he said. But after he answered me, he had to bite his lip to hold back the tears.

10

THE SEVENTY-TWO-HOUR WINDOW

I HAD NO IDEA what was being said or written about me during the first few days after my catastrophic injury. I didn't know anything about the important "seventy-two-hour window" during which it was critical that I showed improvement, nor was I aware that my Rutgers teammates decided to show their support by having stickers attached to the front of their helmets. Their one-word message to the world: BELIEVE.

All this was happening outside my hospital room, a world that seemed like it was a million miles away. I had more important things on my mind, like when I would regain use of my limbs. I thought feelings and sensation would return any moment—or that I'd wake up from this bad dream. My spirits remained high as my new reality set in, partly because I truly believed I would walk again. I figured all I needed was a double dose of patience and time to allow my body to rebound from such a massive hit.

I really don't remember anything before Wednesday, when I recall Mom bending over me, her sad eyes looking into mine. I was uncomfortable with a breathing tube down my throat as well as a feeding tube. Monitors filled the ICU with white noise.

Relief washed over me. Mom was there at my darkest hour.

"I'll be back," I croaked.

"Yes, you'll surprise everyone," she said.

But then we received a wallop of bad news that Wednesday afternoon. Mom told me that my doctors were greatly concerned about my ability to breathe. They wanted to cut a hole into my windpipe, or trachea, and insert a tube that was connected to a ventilator to supply oxygen to my lungs. After the operation, called a tracheotomy, I heard familiar voices speaking—Mom and Rheanne. I tried to get their attention by clucking my tongue.

Rheanne drew close. "Yes! I'm here!"

"Will you help me walk again?" I managed to press out.

She flashed that great smile of hers. "Yes, I will help you walk again."

Hearing that, my thought was, *Good, we got this*.

The ventilator made it difficult to talk, so I quickly lost tolerance for the machine that assisted my breathing. The thing itched like crazy and made a terrible racket each time the ventilator inhaled and exhaled for me. The noise made sleep impossible. I was also worried that the ventilator tube would fall out and no one would be around to connect the apparatus to the opening of my windpipe.

As for regaining movement in my arms and legs or experiencing any sensation below my neck, nothing was happening on that front. My mom and Rutgers University decided to let the important seventy-two-hour marker pass without commenting publicly on my condition.

These were the first few days of the rest of my life. Now that I was gaining an awareness of my surroundings, I couldn't get my head around what had happened. I didn't accept the enormity of my injury—at least not yet. I mean, I knew I had received a horrible neck fracture on the football field. I also understood that I would never have the same life as before, but that's about as far as I got in my thinking.

Air Lift

Every night that first week, we had a late visitor: Coach Schiano. He would arrive by helicopter around eleven o'clock and maintain a vigil for a couple of hours. Throughout the year, Coach had a helicopter at his disposal so that he could save time traveling around New Jersey for recruiting and speaking engagements. It took him about nine minutes to fly from Rutgers to Hackensack, a trip that could take up to two hours if the turnpike was backed up.

I don't know how he had time to see me, because once our visit was over, he flew back to New Brunswick, drove home, grabbed a few hours of sleep, then got up and presided over early morning team meetings, which started at seven fifteen. Football practice then followed.

We grew very close from those late-night visits, and Coach Schiano became a lot more than a coach to me.

Angels in My Presence

Everything was new those first few weeks at Hackensack—my surroundings, my nurses and doctors, the smells and sounds, and the commotion. I hadn't come to grips with what had happened on the twenty-five-yard line during the Rutgers-Army game.

While I was in ICU, a nurse named Angelique sensed that Mom had nothing left to give and said she'd pinch-hit for her. "You get some rest," Angelique told Mom. "I'll stay with Eric and won't leave him." The nurse rubbed my head until I fell asleep, and true to her word, she was still with me at seven thirty in the morning when Mom returned.

My sister, Nicole, and Auntie Cheryl took time off from work to be by my side. I liked having my older sister in the vicinity, because she had a unique talent: She could read my lips better than anyone else. I'd try to speak a few words, and Mom would say, "What's he saying? What's he saying?"

Nicole, from across the room, would say, "Oh, Mom. He's saying 'I'm hungry.'"

I was fed through a feeding tube because my doctors wanted to see how liquids were going down my throat. They wanted to be sure everything was going straight to my stomach and not into my lungs.

I wasn't ready for real food yet—that kind of swallow test would come several weeks later. But for now, my doctors were vitally interested in how my throat was working—and whether the surgery to straighten my fractured vertebrae would be successful.

This was a big deal, because my doctors were intimating to Mom that I might never be able to eat solid foods again.

Mom didn't let me hear about those discussions because she wanted me to focus on getting better, figuring we could deal with the eating issue down the road. In the meantime, Mom knew that I'd be greatly interested in watching Rutgers's next football game, which was on the first Friday night of my hospital stay. The Scarlet Knights had won the first five out of seven games, and we were looking to keep it going against the University of Pittsburgh Panthers on the road.

It wasn't long before the cameras focused on a Rutgers player with a shiny BELIEVE sticker attached to the front of his helmet. It was great to see the support I had from Rutgers and Pittsburgh fans and players, even though we ended up losing that game.

From the moment I spun and hit the turf in New Meadowlands Stadium, I was making an impact on people's lives all across the country and bonded with the New

Jersey football community. Thousands of people were moved by what had happened and went out of their way to write me letters of encouragement. Many were addressed, "Eric LeGrand, Rutgers Football Team, New Jersey," but they still found their way to my hospital bed. Nicole used to sit in my room and read them to me by the dozens.

Letters even came through official channels from such head coaches as Bill Belichick of the New England Patriots, Joe Paterno at Penn State, and Lane Kiffin with the USC Trojans. Hearing Nicole read their words of encouragement meant a great deal to me as well.

Two NFL head coaches—Tom Coughlin of the New York Giants and Andy Reid of the Philadelphia Eagles—even dropped by Hackensack to deliver their encouragement *in person*. I had seen them on television many times before, but actually meeting and talking with them was a thrill.

Many people wanted to offer a more tangible form of support, and to meet that demand, Rutgers helped Mom establish the Eric LeGrand Believe Fund as a collection point for the money donations coming in from many directions.

But what I appreciated just as much, if not more,

were nonmonetary displays of support. Within a few days of my injury, Scott Kaye and Mike Frauenheim, both sales representatives for Riddell, a sporting apparel company, came up with a plan to donate sixteen thousand number 52 helmet decals to as many New Jersey high school football teams as they could. Just mapping out the driving routes to get all the stickers to the teams was quite a logistical effort. And Steve Ostergren of Scarlet Fever, a Rutgers fan shop in New Brunswick, had scarlet-red T-shirts with ERIC BELIEVE NO. 52 printed on the front and KEEP CHOPPING on the back. Actions like these, along with the variety of fundraisers and shows of support in the coming months, would help to keep my spirits high. And the "Believe" story took a life of its own and became the motto for the Rutgers football team after my injury. Beginning with the Pittsburgh game, the offense broke every huddle with a handclap and chanting "Believe!" in unison.

Coach Schiano, Aunt Cheryl, Uncle Ariel, and team chaplain John Maurer would become another important source of support for me—a spiritual support. My aunt and uncle were strong Christians who took their faith seriously and were heavily involved with their church. As for Coach Schiano, he had always worn his Christian faith on his coaching sleeve. He liked to joke that without his faith he never would have gotten through his first few years at Rutgers when the team was losing so many games, but he saw coaching as a way to impact players' lives—almost as a ministry.

We shared powerful times of prayer during some of my darkest moments, when I was confronted with a pessimistic prognosis that I might never walk again. I'll never forget the times when Aunt Cheryl, Uncle Ariel, and Coach Schiano would gather around my hospital bed and pray out loud to God to work a special miracle in my life and heal me.

A few days after my surgery, Aunt Cheryl asked if she could read Psalm 23 to me. I could barely move my head, so I was nearly immobilized. I needed hope during a time of despair.

She opened her Bible and read these centuries-old words, which soothed my troubled soul:

> *The Lord is my shepherd, I lack nothing.*
> *He makes me lie down in green pastures, he leads me beside quiet waters, he refreshes my soul. He guides me along the right paths for his name's sake.*
> *Even though I walk through the darkest valley, I will fear no evil, for you are with me; your rod and your staff, they comfort me.*

You prepare a table before me in the presence of my enemies. You anoint my head with oil; my cup overflows.
Surely your goodness and love will follow me all the days of my life, and I will dwell in the house of the Lord forever.

Those sentences lifted my spirits, especially the part about walking through the darkest valley. That's where I was—the darkest valley. It didn't get any darker, if you asked me. But the psalmist reminded me that the Lord was with me and his rod and his staff comforted me.

I couldn't help but be struck by the irony of the use of the word "walk" through the darkest valley. There I was, lying in a hospital bed in ICU, hooked up to every kind of machine there was, and I couldn't walk at all. I wasn't regaining any feeling or the ability to move any muscles below my neck.

When you lie in a hospital bed every waking moment, you have a lot of time to think.

A lot of deep thoughts were going through my mind, like:

Why did this injury happen to me?

Why did God allow this to happen to me?

What did I do wrong?

I had some awesome conversations with John Maurer, discussing heavy questions on my mind. I was not angry with God. Confused, yes. But not angry. My mind constantly played with the what-ifs:

- What if the kickoff had veered off to the right instead of to the left?
- What if those blockers had succeeded in bottling me up and keeping me away from the return man?
- What if I'd hit Malcolm Brown a little differently and not with the tip of my helmet?

John told me that the Lord had not forsaken me, that he knew exactly where I was and what I was dealing with, and God never does anything by accident, even in a tragedy like I had experienced. God's thoughts were not our thoughts, John said. He had a plan for my life, and unfortunately, this pain and suffering was part of it. Our discussions helped me come to a place where all I could do was trust in God . . . trust him for the outcome.

God still cared about me, still had a plan for my life. He had not abandoned me on that football field. I decided that the greatest thing I had going was to trust in God's plan, whatever it was.

11

MAKING THE MOVE TO KESSLER

AFTER ABOUT THREE WEEKS at Hackensack, the doctors began discussing my future. Mom huddled up with Nicole and Aunt Cheryl to discuss my options. They were told to check out the Kessler Institute for Rehabilitation in West Orange, New Jersey.

During their tour, Mom, Nicole, and Aunt Cheryl learned that Kessler was where actor Christopher Reeve spent the first six months of recovery after an excruciating fall left him a quadriplegic.

I hadn't watched any Superman movies growing up,

but Mom and my family members had, and they told me Christopher Reeve was quite the Superman onscreen and off. Talented and good-looking, he was a superb athlete who did his own stunts. He was an expert sailor, scuba diver, and skier. By the 1990s, he had found a new passion: riding horses. He loved to compete in show-jumping events.

In May 1995, Christopher was riding his Thorough-bred, Eastern Express, through a course when the horse suddenly balked at a rail jump, pitching him forward. His hands got tangled in the horse's bridle, and he landed headfirst, fracturing the uppermost vertebrae in his spine and instantly paralyzing him from the neck down.

During my family's tour of Kessler, they were impressed with a large, airy, gymlike wing where spinal cord injury victims went through their rehabilitation exercises. Kessler was one of only seven centers in the United States with a rehabilitation program like this.

When Mom returned, she told me some good news. "Kessler can take you in a few days," she said.

"But I don't know if I'm ready," I replied. I mean, I wanted to get better, but as an athlete, I knew I needed to regroup before I took things to the next level.

"But sweetie, the faster you start rehab, the faster you

can regain the use of your arms and legs."

I didn't know what to say. I knew deep down that my body wasn't ready. I needed more rest. This wasn't the right time.

Nobody was hearing me, or even if they were, they thought they knew better. Both my sister and aunt chimed in about how great Kessler was going to be.

On the way to Kessler, something inside my stomach went crazy, and I felt nauseated. I certainly wasn't myself.

Rutgers Travels to Florida

After getting settled into my room at Kessler, my mood improved when the Rutgers football game came on at eight later that evening. Mom, Rheanne, and Nicole were planning to watch with me. My teammates would be playing the University of South Florida on ESPN. This would be one of those unusual Wednesday night games.

As the game wore on, though, I became more agitated and had no patience for anything, including the TV timeouts.

Rheanne noticed there was something off about me. "Eric, what's wrong with you?" she said. "You need to relax."

How can I chill? Doesn't she know there's a strong

possibility I'll never walk again? This was a thought that rarely crossed my mind—and something I didn't believe. But I also was not in denial. When this fleeting thought came to mind, I would focus on the positive. Focus on my faith and my plans—God's plans for my life. But on this particular night, I couldn't seem to shake my attitude. I didn't feel like myself.

In the fourth quarter of the game, whether it was the lateness of the hour—it was nearing midnight—or my frustration with how the game was playing out, I fell asleep. Rheanne and Nicole were feeling sleepy too, so they headed out.

Right before the South Florida game finished (a game we would lose), I woke up and started acting weird. My eyes were so scary-looking that Mom shook me and slapped me lightly in the face. But I didn't respond. She felt as though I was looking right through her.

"Eric, snap out of it!" she said.

"Hit me again," I said in my delirium. My body felt like it was on fire, and in my feverishness, I had no idea Mom was yelling at me to get a grip. "Eric, calm down!" said the voice I didn't recognize.

The next thing I knew, I was on a stretcher and being

wheeled down a long hallway. I tried to train my eyes on what was happening around me, but it felt like I was looking at the world through fogged-out goggles. And my body was so warm.

Mom was walking beside me. I asked her a question. "Am I cross-eyed, Mom?"

"No, but you need to close your eyes," she replied. My eyes *were* cross-eyed, so much so that she thought my eyes would pop out of my skull any moment.

I kept trying to move my arms. Why didn't they move? And my hands? Why couldn't I twiddle my fingers?

More efforts to move my arms drew on all the strength and exertion I'd once had, but nothing would happen. And then I blacked out. Mercifully.

I woke up in an emergency room. I was behind a partitioned curtain with my mother and sister. I recognized both of them. (Mom had called Nicole, who had come straight back immediately.)

"Hey, Nicole, are we going to IHOP today?" I always liked going to the International House of Pancakes growing up. They had great pancakes and waffles.

"What's wrong with you?" Nicole demanded.

"I want to go to IHOP. I feel like pancakes."

173

"Eric, go back to sleep."

"No." I tried to get up, but I couldn't. Nicole had to be sitting on me, just like she did when I was a kindergartener. "Get off me right," I said.

"Eric, I'm not on you."

"Get off of me! I want to get out of here!"

I put my head down and allowed myself to fall into a daze.

A high fever had made me irrational. My body temperature had spiked to 105.5 degrees—half a degree from frying my brain. I was told later that high fevers were common for someone in my condition.

News that I had been rushed to Saint Barnabas was treated as a setback by the media. It was a scary situation for twelve hours, but I eventually came around.

Everything will be okay, I told myself. Just as I tell myself today that my accident had a higher purpose, I now believe that incident happened for a reason. Several days at Saint Barnabas helped me find new perspective.

I was alive. I didn't die on the football field. I had survived. I recognized that even though I lay on a hospital bed, unable to move anything below my neck, I was still blessed. I still had things to be thankful for, and number one on the list was being alive. I had a family who loved me *and* wanted me to live. I had a Creator who knew exactly what I was going through.

Five days later, I was transferred back to Kessler with a newfound outlook. I also got into a better frame of mind—a frame of mind that I had to have the same mental toughness I showed on the football field.

Mental toughness.

That was probably the strongest attribute I developed while playing football, and I knew I'd now have to draw on my mental strength like never before.

Learning Curve

One of the mental challenges of becoming paralyzed was getting my head around the idea that I would not be able to take care of myself.

That was really hard—and is still the most difficult aspect of my life today. Take a simple thing like an itching nose. Before the injury, I'd rub my nose with one of my fingers and that would take care of the itch. Now I had to scrunch up my nose, wiggle my mouth, and stretch my facial muscles to satisfy the itch, but usually those actions didn't cut it. That's when I would ask Mom to draw closer so that I could rub my face against her arm or shoulder.

But if nobody was close enough to scratch my nose, a

simple thing like a facial itch could be agony.

Everything was a learning curve, including getting used to my new motorized wheelchair. The high-tech Permobil C500 came with a molded plastic mouthpiece that I could use to move around as I desired. Pressing the mouthpiece upward with my lips moved the wheelchair forward, while a nudge on either side would turn the wheelchair in any direction I wanted. Pressing *down* on the mouthpiece with my lips or chin stopped the wheelchair. You can only imagine how sensitive the mouthpiece is to the direction of my lips.

It took some practice getting used to moving around, but I had plenty of time to get the hang of it. It was a wonderful feeling to get some measure of independence back.

I also was eager to do rehab. My therapists told me that their goal was to help me regain as much function as possible. To accomplish that, they would use methods to help my spinal column "remap" connections to my arms and legs, which meant physically retraining the legs and the trunk while reawakening the nervous system. I set the bar higher: I wanted to walk again, but I understood that to get there, I first needed to regain motor function and sensation.

I had a responsibility to give rehab my best effort, just as I had had a responsibility on the football field. How could I let down the thousands of people behind me—those praying for me, those encouraging me, and those financially supporting the Believe Fund?

I knew that I had a job to do, and that was to get myself healthy. The first order of business was to get off the ventilator, which made me very uncomfortable. It was one thing to lie in a bed and not be able to move, but dealing with a ventilator contributed to my misery. I didn't like the way the ventilator made it harder to talk. I didn't like the noise it made at night, which kept me awake. And I was still nervous that my vent would pop off and I wouldn't be able to breathe.

I hated the ventilator so much that one time I told my pulmonary nurse that I didn't need it anymore a month after my injury. She spoke with my pulmonary doctor, Dr. Douglas Green, but they were both hesitant to take me off the ventilator because they didn't think my lungs were strong enough to carry the load. I felt going off the vent *would* make my lungs stronger, so I made my case to them. I believe I changed their minds because they saw the look of determination on my face.

"We can take you off the vent and see how you'll do," the nurse said after consulting the doctor, "but you'll be lucky to last a minute."

I took that as a challenge. The first time they shut down the ventilator, I went for an hour and a half breathing on my own. The next time, I went two hours...then a half day. I was breathing fine. When I get something into my head, I'll do whatever it takes to follow through, and in this situation, I was going to will myself off the vent. A few days before Thanksgiving, I was taken off the ventilator for good. Score one for the home team.

12

REACHING OUT TO THE PUBLIC

FOR THE NEXT THREE months, I continued daily rehab at Kessler. I would do different exercises that helped improve my sitting posture in the wheelchair, because I was working my upper body, core muscles, and back muscles.

Throughout the month of March, I had made so much progress that doctors removed my tracheotomy and my medical team told Mom that we should start thinking about checking out and moving back home. I could continue physical therapy on an outpatient basis three times a week at Kessler in West Orange or any Kessler satellite facility.

Aunt Cheryl and Uncle Ariel heard the news and knew that we couldn't return to my house, because it was not going to be possible to get around in the wheelchair. They offered to open their home until we figured out our plan. They lived in Jackson, a township in the center of the Garden State. At the end of March, I was ready to leave Kessler. Fortunately, we had great transportation to get there. Thanks to NCAA insurance, Mom purchased a brand-new, wheelchair-accessible Volkswagen Routan minivan. The van was equipped with a motorized ramp and a system to lock in my wheelchair to the floorboard.

Aunt Cheryl and Uncle Ariel created a wonderful atmosphere for me, and I loved the closeness of family. What a difference that made in our lives. I was home again and ready to take on the rest of my recovery with a newfound energy.

Since then, I've resumed my college education by taking classes online. My first course online was a class at Rutgers called Blacks in Economics. I watched it in real time, through Skype, and wrote papers on my laptop using voice-recognition software. There was a steep learning curve, since I could no longer type with my fingers, but I gained confidence as I learned how to tell my computer what words I wanted on the screen.

I also learned that I could touch people through my computer. I opened a Twitter account (@EricLeGrand52) after I moved to Jackson, with a goal of posting something every day or two using voice-recognition software. It was fun to watch the number of followers rise quickly . . . a thousand the first week, five thousand within a month, and then I hit the ten-thousand mark in the summer of 2011. These days, I have more than sixty thousand Twitter followers, and I sometimes tweet several times a day.

My Facebook page (EricLeGrand52) has taken off as well, and today I have more than fifty-five thousand friends. Through my frequent messages, I can inspire my virtual friends and fans as well as keep them up-to-date with what I'm doing.

In a quest to leave no technological stone unturned, when people try to call me on my cell and the call goes to voice mail, they will hear the following message:

Hey, how are you doing? This is Eric LeGrand. I want to leave you with a quick message before you go. Never take anything for granted. Each day is a gift. It is a prize of its own. You have to go out there and receive it and enjoy it

to the best of your abilities. That's what I do every day of my life.
And always remember: Believe.

I love inspiring others and look forward to using today's technology to spread the message of hope.

One exciting thing about the public nature of my injury is how it has resulted in invitations to meet some important people and local professional teams.

New Jersey governor Chris Christie asked my family and me to come to the statehouse in Trenton. And after we met the governor, three New York sports teams opened their doors to me during the summer: the New York Jets, the New York Mets, and the New York Yankees. I got to meet some amazing people, like LaDainian Tomlinson, who momentarily left me tongue-tied. He used to play for the San Diego Chargers and ran well against my favorite team, the Denver Broncos, but I couldn't help but feel starstruck when he introduced himself. I also met Jets linebacker Bart Scott for the first time. Unbelievable.

And when I visited the Yankees, I got to hang out with such great stars as Derek Jeter, Alex Rodriguez, Brett Gardner, and manager Joe Girardi.

In between those incredible experiences, I kept

grinding away at Kessler. It was the middle of the summer when I tweeted a photo of myself standing up with the assistance of a special metallized frame at Kessler. "Standing tall, we can't fall," I dictated to my voice-activated iPhone. After another session, I tweeted "45 minutes of standing today, it's a whole new world being up at my height again."

Behind the Mike

Just before the start of Rutgers's 2011 season, Coach called with an exciting proposition: "How would you like to become part of the Rutgers radio broadcast team?"

Coach didn't have to ask twice. "Really? I can't believe it."

"Believe it," Coach said.

He explained that I could offer my "expert analysis" in the pregame, halftime, and postgame reports, all from a player's perspective. "You'll be our E-rock report," Coach said.

Once again, a wonderful thing was happening to me. I had always wanted to play in the NFL and become a broadcaster after I retired from the game, and here was a chance to get my feet wet in a broadcast setting that I was entirely comfortable with. God's plan at work, I thought on hearing the news. This would be an opportunity to live out one of my dreams, even if the circumstances weren't as I would have ever imagined.

I was worried about doing a good job, and I'm indebted to veteran broadcaster Chris Carlin, who is the radio play-by-play voice of Rutgers football. Chris met with me several times before the season and showed me how to handle things inside the broadcast booth and what makes a good analyst.

I would be working with Chris's sidekick, Marc Malusis. Marc was an old pro, and he quickly put me at ease. He would recap what had happened on the field, run through the stats, and then ask me at halftime what adjustments had to be made or during the postgame show what the Scarlet Knights had to work on for their next opponent. Fan feedback was great. People I ran into said they liked hearing my voice on the radio and what I had to say because I knew the players so well.

October Surprise

I couldn't wait for October 29 to arrive—I had planned with Coach Schiano to lead the team out onto the football field that day for the West Virginia game. But on the morning of Saturday, October 29, Mom came into my bedroom and opened the curtains.

"See the snow?" Mom asked.

I looked out. It was snowing, all right. Actually, it was nasty outside. A big storm had deposited an inch or two of the white stuff on the ground. Even in New Jersey, an October snowstorm was surprising.

"So what are we going to do?" Mom continued. "Are you sure you want to do this?"

"This is perfect," I said. "With all the adversity I've been through, how can I not go ahead?" After the events of a little more than a year ago, I knew I could handle a little snow.

I wasn't so sure about the cold, however. My body always felt chilled, even if I was indoors with the heat on. I would be outside for a long time. There was no way I could avoid being cold today.

When we arrived at the stadium, it was freezing outside. We parked near the Rutgers locker room underneath the south grandstands so that I could see the guys before the game, especially my old roommate Scott Vallone. "You're still part of the team," he said, which was nice to hear. I especially enjoyed taking in the musty smell of the locker room through my nostrils,

185

including the minty aroma of liniment.

Mom took me to the press box, where Marc Malusis and I did the pregame show. We talked about how Rutgers had started the season strong, winning five out of the first six games, but an unexpected 16-14 loss to Louisville the week before left the team with a 5-2 record and 2-1 in the Big East Conference.

I noted that West Virginia was bringing another strong team to Piscataway: the Mountaineers were the twenty-fifth-ranked team in the country, with a similar 5-2 record but 1-1 in conference play. The feeling among the players, however, was that nobody beats Rutgers seventeen straight times.

When the pregame show was over, Mom and I took the elevator to ground level, and I got in the VW van for the short ride over to the Rutgers locker room. It was rush, rush, rush to get there in time. There were stairs between the locker room and the tunnel leading out to the field, however, so I had to wait inside the tunnel until my teammates came out for me to lead them onto the playing field.

Inside the locker room, Coach Schiano was doing a fine job putting the players in the right frame of mind.

"Big game, gentlemen," he said. "You know the stakes, and you know Eric asked that this be the one game he leads us out. Let's win it for him!"

Meanwhile, I was shivering in the cold. I never thought about wearing a jacket—not at a moment like this. Instead, I had on a long-sleeve Nike Cold Gear thermal T-shirt covered by my black Rutgers jersey, number 52. I had on a red wool cap and gray gloves, but they didn't do much at all to ward off the cold.

When my teammates exited the locker room, my heart pounded with excitement. For the first time in a long time, I forgot how cold it was.

A red-handled ax was placed across my armrests to show our fans that I was still "chopping." Scott Vallone and another old roommate, Khaseem Greene, each grabbed hold of one end of the ax as we moved forward. Coach Schiano cleared a path and then let me come out of the tunnel first.

The Rutgers fans—many of them wearing yellow raincoats or plastic slickers to protect themselves from the wet snow—exploded with cheers as the Rutgers band played our fight song. Then chants of "Fifty-two! Fifty-two!" gained steam as I led a slow procession of teammates onto the field and toward the fifty-yard line. Scott and Khaseem, along with Devon Watkis and Beau Bachety, made sure I didn't get stuck in the snow.

As we rolled out, I wanted to drink in the moment. It had been a little more than a year since I'd last walked onto the field. Today I was rolling in with a new purpose. I didn't even feel the icy flakes hitting my face. I looked at the crowd and thought about the journey I had taken over the last year.

When we reached the fifty-yard line, we made a right turn toward the Rutgers bench. At our sideline, my teammates gathered around me for a final pregame huddle. Coach Schiano was in the middle of the scrum, and he bowed his head. "God, please heal this man!" he cried out. "Please let him walk again!"

"Amen!" the team said in unison.

Coach then broke us with his familiar chant: "It's family on three . . . one-two-three—family!"

The crowd cheered crazily as I exited the field, but from the corner of my eye I witnessed two of my teammates crying—Brandon Jones and Steve Beauharnais. That's when I almost lost it, too, but I was becoming numb from the cold.

Mom took me back to the van, where I warmed up again. Then we returned to the press box, where I did an interview with ABC before joining Marc Malusis for the halftime show in the broadcast booth.

When Marc and I were done breaking down the first half, I wheeled myself into a nearby suite, where Mom and some family members were watching the game. She could see that I was still freezing. Mom wrapped me in everything she could find: two blankets, a sweatshirt, and a hat. But I was still powerfully cold, and nothing could warm me up. Once you get a chill like that, it's a deep-to-the-bone chill, and it takes hours for the body to regulate and warm back up.

The game didn't go too well; once again, Rutgers lost to West Virginia. I was upset but not too troubled, because I was more worried about staying warm. If it had been a nice, sunny day, I would have been much more upset than I was.

Mom drove us back to our apartment after the game, my teeth chattering and my body involuntarily shivering even though Mom had the heat blasting into my face. Back in July, we had moved from Auntie Cheryl and Uncle Ariel's home to a wheelchair-accessible apartment in Woodbridge, which borders my hometown of Avenel. The move brought us closer to Kessler, closer to our community support, and closer to Rutgers.

I finally warmed up just before we arrived, but when I had to go from the parking lot of our apartment complex into our unit, I got chilled all over again.

When we were finally inside the apartment, Mom took off my wet clothes, dressed me for bed, and put two blankets over my head. I shivered for a long time, and I wasn't warm until five o'clock in the morning, when my body finally regulated. It was a miserable night. Just miserable.

I didn't stay down for long, though—not after the reception I had received the day before. My spirits picked up the next day, and I tweeted this message: "So I left tire tracks in the snow yesterday as I led my team out next time will be footprints."

But God had something planned that I never could have predicted.

Sports Moment of the Year

Like most rambunctious boys growing up, I wasn't the biggest reader, but I did like to thumb through *Sports*

Illustrated. The stories were always informative, and the photography was always amazing.

A month after I led my team onto the field at Rutgers, *Sports Illustrated* announced that for the first time ever in its fifty-seven-year history, the editor would not be choosing the image that would go on the cover of the magazine. Instead, *SI* would let the fans choose the Best Sports Moment of 2011 for the cover of the year-end double issue. They could vote on Facebook—there were fifteen moments to choose from. I guess some of the editors had seen the media about me leading the team out onto the field against West Virginia; anyway, it was one of the choices. The image that received the most votes by December 16 would appear on the cover.

There were many great moments to choose from— ace quarterback Aaron Rodgers leading Green Bay to victory in Super Bowl XLV, a monster dunk by the Clippers' Blake Griffin, and Derek Jeter becoming the first Yankee to reach three thousand hits. Seeing my competition, I figured that I didn't have a chance.

But then I received some help from unexpected sources. New Jersey governor Chris Christie and Newark mayor Cory Booker started tweeting about me and urged New Jersey residents in particular and football fans everywhere to vote for me. After that, my vote counts went crazy.

Several days before the December 16 deadline, *Sports Illustrated* closed down the results tab so that nobody could see what was going on. I could barely contain my excitement, because I knew I had a good chance to be the Best Sports Moment of 2011. I thought it would really be a cool thing to win, but I didn't get my hopes sky-high or anything.

On the day *Sports Illustrated* would announce the winner, I had been asked to interview Coach Schiano for Sports New York—the first time I was doing broadcast work for a regional sports channel seen throughout the Northeast. Rutgers had bounced back with another excellent season in 2011, finishing 8-4, so there was a lot to talk about. The interview time was set for twelve thirty at the Hale Center.

I was chitchatting with the producer and camera people before Coach's arrival when I noticed two people standing nearby.

"Who are they?" I asked.

"Oh, they're with Rutgers Radio," said the producer.

"They're here to listen to your interview with Coach Schiano."

Mom entered the team meeting room. By this time, it was ten minutes after twelve, and the winner of *SI*'s Best Moment of the Year had been announced.

"Mom, can you show me my phone? I want to see if I won."

"Oh, I forgot it in the van," she replied. "Do you want me to get it?"

Did I want her to get it? Of course I did. "Mom, I want to know if I won."

"Okay. I'll be right back," she said.

Mom turned on her heels and left the team meeting room as Coach Schiano was entering. It was time to do my interview; I guessed I would have to wait a little longer, although the suspense was killing me.

The producer sat Coach down, the lighting was adjusted, and off we went—the tape was rolling.

After I was done, I was making small talk with Coach Schiano when I noticed Mom leave the team meeting room and return a minute later with a poster in her hand.

"What's that, Mom?" I asked as she approached us.

She gave me a bright smile and turned the poster in

her right hand. What I saw nearly made me faint. The poster was a giant *Sports Illustrated* cover—a picture of me coming out of the Rutgers tunnel, surrounded by my teammates. FANS' CHOICE said the headline, with a subhead of THE RETURN OF ERIC LEGRAND.

"Eric, you won!" Mom screamed. Just then a half dozen reporters and photographers poured into the team meeting room, and I heard the clicks of cameras and blinked from the flashes. They started asking me all sorts of questions, and now I was the one having to come up with answers.

The two guys who were with Rutgers Radio? They were actually from *Sports Illustrated*. Turns out my mother knew everything the day before, but she didn't tell me I had won. She normally wasn't very good at keeping a secret, but I guess she was able to keep this one, because I had no idea.

I wanted to do an end-zone dance but settled for a big whoop-de-do holler. Coach Schiano looked happier than I was. The *Sports Illustrated* representatives said I captured 29 percent of the vote total, 10 percent higher than second-place finisher Lionel Messi, the Argentine soccer star. Seventy-nine-million people from 119 countries cast votes online for me. That was insane.

Gracing the cover of *Sports Illustrated* meant the world to me. It really did. That is something you dream about as a little kid—achieving something remarkable in the world of sports and receiving recognition for that moment from the most influential sports magazine in the world.

I was in awe and didn't know what to say.

13

TOUCHING PEOPLE'S LIVES

PUBLIC SPEAKING IS A high-wire act at times, but even if there isn't a net below me, I still like to get up in front of audiences and inspire people. I started sharing my story in the fall of 2011 when Jersey City Middle School 7 gym teacher Alan Gross called and asked if I would say something to the students. Up until then, my public speaking had been limited to saying a "few words" while visiting my teammates at the Hale Center. Going to Jersey City Middle School 7 would be my first honest-to-goodness "speaking" event before a live audience larger than a few people.

"I don't blame God, or Malcolm Brown, the player at Army, or anyone else for what happened," I said in my speech. "I now see life from a different perspective. I see that there is more to life than football practice, going to the weight room, study sessions, and playing in games. I think that's a good thing."

When I described the kickoff play—how I had zeroed in on Malcolm Brown only to go down, paralyzed—you could hear a pin drop. The middle schoolers hung on every word, and I think it's because most kids have never been around someone in a wheelchair. They'd never seen anyone talk honestly about the circumstances that landed him there.

When I finished taking a few questions, the students were dismissed. I was still on the stage when I noticed a sixth-grade boy using a mobility cane in his right hand to mount the three steps.

He continued tapping and coming in my direction, and when he reached me, he asked if he could ask me a question.

"Of course."

"I'm blind," he said. "What advice do you have for somebody with a disability like me?"

"You have to believe in yourself," I replied. "You can't

let anything stop you from being the best you can be, from being yourself. You have a lot going for you. You can talk, and you can think, so let me leave you with that encouragement."

I could see that my words touched this young boy, but he touched me as well. Connecting with this boy and others like him has helped me realize that my own struggles are not in vain.

I've since spoken at dozens and dozens of schools, either in the classroom or schoolwide assemblies. I always include a question-and-answer time when I'm done. "Go ahead, don't be scared," I'll say. "You can ask me anything."

These days, whether it's an encounter with a blind boy or a speaking engagement in front of a thousand people in a ballroom, I remind everyone to believe in themselves, believe in the Man Above, and believe anything is truly possible, because I believe anything is possible.

Speaking Up

A quarter of a million people in the United States live with spinal cord injuries, with half paraplegic and the other half quadriplegic. (Paraplegics are paralyzed in the lower half of the body and quadriplegics from the neck down.) There are an estimated ten thousand to twelve thousand spinal cord injuries every year in the United States, according to the National Spinal Cord Injury Statistical Center.

More than half of all spinal cord injuries occur between the ages of sixteen and thirty, and more than 80 percent of those who experience spinal cord injuries are male. They haven't received even a thimbleful of the support that I have, and I would imagine that the vast majority have been forgotten by everyone except their close family.

They weren't injured while playing an NCAA college football game broadcast on ESPN3, because you can count on two hands the number of spinal cord injuries that come from playing football each year at the professional, college, and high school level. Around 40 percent of all spinal cord injuries are the result of motor vehicle accidents, and the rest generally come from falls or violent acts, like stabbings or gunshot wounds.

Many are sent home from the hospital in a push wheelchair with not much else but wishes of good luck. My situation is different because I had three different insurance plans covering my Permobil C500 wheelchair, the VW Routan wheelchair-accessible van, and the restorative therapy bike, as well as the micro-AIR mattress, the mat table, and electrical stimulation devices. What I'm especially grateful for is that we have insurance to pay for the daily nursing care that comes to our home. Each day, a registered nurse comes to our place for three hours and a nurse's aide for eight hours. Mom and I need every minute these angels are with us, because it takes between two and three hours to get me ready each morning. It's quite a lot of work—much more than my mother could ever handle.

As you might imagine, it's really hard for me to travel, since I need so much care. But then some of my Colonia High friends started talking about taking a spring break trip to Miami in the spring of 2012. When they excitedly described their plans for a four-day trip, I said they could count me in. I had always wanted to go to Miami for a vacation. I knew I'd love being in a place where I wasn't shivering every time I went outside.

Plans were made, and flights were booked. Mom had to buy a portable air mattress because I couldn't sleep in a regular bed; otherwise I'd get pressure sores. The portable air mattress wasn't cheap, but we could use it for future travels. And we also had to rent a handicap-accessible van to get around . . . I'm telling you, there was a lot of planning for a four-day beach vacation, but we sure had a great time—and gave Mom a break.

My spring break vacation could have been one of those promotions for MasterCard:

Airfare from Newark to Miami: $509
Dinner and drinks at the Clevelander: $40
Talking with Lil Wayne at Club LIV and always feeling warm for four days: priceless

14

SIGNING BONUS

In the lead-up to the 2012 NFL draft in late April, two ESPN analysts were in regular rotation: draft experts Mel Kiper Jr. and Todd McShay. The duo makes for great television, because they often disagree and their banter is quite entertaining. They can be blistering in their opinions and love to talk up or talk down each player on their "big board"—the first round of the draft.

As I watched the pair jabber on and on about the NFL draft, it was easy for me to daydream about what might have been. . . . Coach Schiano had left Rutgers in

January 2012 to become the head coach of the Tampa Bay Buccaneers, and it was fun to dream that I could have followed him there as an NFL player.

You see, 2012 would have been my draft year, and playing in the NFL had been my dream since my Pop Warner days in Avenel. I imagined hearing my name announced and walking out of the greenroom and being handed a team hat and receiving a bear hug from NFL Commissioner Roger Goodell.

But that wasn't going to happen. As I watched player after player stride onto the Radio City Music Hall stage for a grip-and-grin with the commissioner, I became really homesick for football. I missed playing a game I had grown to love.

I would never get my chance, but at least Coach Schiano would get a chance to prove himself as an NFL coach. I was particularly interested in what moves Coach would make during the draft. The Bucs had finished the 2011 season with the NFL's longest losing streak, so there were holes in the roster. Coach and his assistants did a lot of maneuvering.

About ten days after the draft, Mom got a phone call from Coach. She was outside Kessler, waiting in the van while I underwent physical therapy.

After exchanging pleasantries, Coach explained the reason for the phone call. "Karen, I want to run this by you first to make sure it's okay. We would like to sign Eric to a free-agent contract with the Bucs."

My mom wasn't sure she'd heard right.

"Are you saying—?"

"Yes, we would like him to be part of the team."

Mom felt overwhelmed. "How could it not be okay?" she asked. "Eric will be absolutely thrilled if you did this."

"Well, we are going to offer Eric a free-agent contract, and I'm going to call him tomorrow, so don't tell him."

"Okay, Coach," she said. "I'll do my best not to tell Eric, but please call him early, because I don't know how long I can hold out."

So I had no inkling what was up when Coach called in a chatty mood the following day. We were talking football when he changed the subject. "I want to sign you as one of our free agents," he blurted.

I didn't think I'd heard right. "Are you serious?" I asked. "You're going to waste a spot on me?" I knew that all NFL teams were limited to a ninety-man roster going into training camp.

"This is something I want to do," Coach replied. "I talked to the GM and our owner, and everyone is on board."

I didn't know what to say except, "Thanks, Coach."

But deep down, I was super, super excited. This was a dream come true. I had always wanted to go to the NFL. It wasn't the circumstances that I wanted, and I knew I would never get on the field, but this gesture from Coach . . . this act of humanity . . . meant the world to me. I also knew this decision would show football fans everywhere what type of person Greg Schiano is—someone who looks out for the welfare of others instead of himself.

Coach said he would send me a team jersey with number 52 and my name on the back as well as a Bucs helmet, and he also invited me to come to Tampa Bay to meet my teammates whenever I wanted.

When the phone call was over, I felt like I could levitate in my wheelchair—or at least do some wheelies. It didn't take long for the Tampa Bay organization to announce the news—including a statement from Coach Schiano saying, "The way Eric lives his life epitomizes what we are looking for in Buccaneer men." He called the signing "a small gesture to recognize his character, spirit, and perseverance."

What does the signing mean in practical terms? There was no money involved, but the team flew me down to Tampa Bay in June during an OTA—that's NFL lingo for "organized team activity"—to watch a practice, meet my teammates, and say a few words to them. Inside the locker room at One Buc Place, my message to the guys was simple: Play every down like it's your last.

15

EXTRA POINT

IT'S HARD TO BELIEVE that it's been nearly two years since that fateful day at the Meadowlands. I find it harder to believe that almost 10 percent of my life has been in a wheelchair.

When I became paralyzed, I knew that many football fans thought my life was over.

They said I'd never shake a hand.

Walk across the street.

Use the remote.

Hold a cheeseburger and take a bite.

207

Brush my teeth.

Grab a shower.

Text a message.

Dial a friend.

Hold an iPad.

Work a jigsaw puzzle.

Walk across a room.

Hold a baby.

Those things—and there are hundreds more I could list—are out of my control. But I can do so much more:

I can make eye contact.

Flash a bright smile.

Have a winning attitude.

Continue to try as hard as I can in rehab.

Share my thoughts in a book.

Watch football games on TV.

Speak words of encouragement.

Tell others that life doesn't end when you face adversity.

Live life to the fullest I am able.

Point people to God.

Those are some of the things I can do and will continue to do in the future.

That's because I believe.

I believe that I will someday get out of this wheelchair and walk again. I believe that I'll stand and shake someone's hand again. I believe that I'll be able to care for myself someday. That belief fuels everything I do.

Whenever I tire during rehab or the mountain looks too high, I remind myself of this singular goal that drives me. Someday, when I can walk again, I want to visit the spot on the Giants Stadium field where I went down. I want to lie on the artificial turf one more time and take a deep breath. Then I'm going to pull myself up to my own feet under my own power and walk away.

Believe it will happen, because I do.

ACKNOWLEDGMENTS

As SOMEONE WITH LIMITED physical movement, I needed a lot of "arms and legs" to make my autobiography happen. First of all, I don't know where I'd be today without my mother, Karen LeGrand, by my side, loving and caring for me with a cheerful attitude. Thanks, Mom, for all you do, and I'll never be able to thank you enough. That's why I dedicated *Believe* to you.

My immediate family has been my bedrock throughout this whole experience. Their love and concern—as well as their investment in my rehabilitation—have meant so much to me. My thanks to:

- my sister, Nicole LeGrand Harrigan, her husband, Kenrick, and their sons, Xavier and Isaac
- my grandmother—or Nana—Betty LeGrand, and my cousin Judyya
- the Curet family: Auntie Cheryl and Uncle Ariel, along with their three children, Jazmin, Aaron, and James
- my father, Donald McCloud, and all my uncles and aunts on his side of the family (Dad had eight brothers and sisters) and my cousins
- my stepsister, Tisha McCloud, and my stepbrothers, Gene and Manny McCloud

My lovely girlfriend, Rheanne Sleiman, gave me her love and support, and it's been great having these friends still there for me: Nate Brown, Joey LaSala, Brandon Hall, Ryan Don Diego, Amir Ahmed, and John and Ray Nevins. Alan Brown and Mike Elchoness have given me great advice since the injury.

When Coach Greg Schiano recruited me to play football for him at Rutgers, he said, "Welcome to the Rutgers family." Coach, you've always been there, just as you said you would. The Rutgers family includes staff and coaches such as Tim Pernetti, Jason Baum, Kevin Mac-Connell, Todd Greineder, Mike Kuzniak, Jay Butler, Robb

Smith, Jeremy Cole, Randy Melvin, and their wives. I'm still teammates for life with Scott Vallone, Beau Bachety, Devon Watkis, Brandon Jones, and Khaseem Greene.

After I was injured against Army, neurosurgeon Dr. Roy Vingan and his medical team saved my life and did everything they could to give me the best possible chance to rehabilitate myself. My ICU nurses at Hackensack University Medical Center, including Angelique, Cherise, and Jen, sat with me during the night and rubbed my head. My physical therapist at Hackensack was Leah.

My inpatient and outpatient therapists at Kessler Institute for Rehabilitation deserve honorable mention for skill and patience: B.J., Buffy, Barbara, Sean, Jerrod, Roxanne, Prashad, Lindsay, Dan, Miriam, and Gabriella. I appreciate Kessler CEO Bonne Evans and my medical team at Kessler: Dr. Monifa Brooks, Dr. Douglas Green, and Dr. Todd Linsenmeyer; my tracheotomy nurse, Rolinda; my nurses Michelle, Mary, Sharon, Ricky, and Maria; Matty, my speech therapist; and my aides Humphrey, George, George, Juice, Harold, Rema, Ariel, Kerry, and Kevin. Gail Solomon helped organize all my media requests while I was at Kessler and continues to do that today.

I had friends in wheelchairs who helped motivate me

while I was at Kessler: Jermaine, Ingrid, Terry, and Mike.

I've gotten to know and work with some great people at the Christopher and Dana Reeve Foundation, including president Peter Wilderotter, senior vice president Maggie Goldberg, and communications coordinator Janelle Lobello.

In the fundraising area, financial planners Kimberly Kingsland and Rhondale Hayward have been a tremendous help with the Eric LeGrand Believe Fund. There's also a special team working behind the scenes with the Eric LeGrand Patriot Saint Foundation, consisting of parents who knew me growing up in Avenel and Woodbridge Township. Jack Nevins, my old Pop Warner coach, quarterbacks a team that includes Millie Shea, Donna Bruno, Michael Shea, Louise Wasyluk, Leigh Farrell, Tom Mangine, and committee members Craig Bruno, Allison Farrell, Tom Farrell, John Farrell, Cathy Herre, Bobby Herre, Kelly Layton, Tracy Mangine, and Harry Smith.

I also want to recognize all the people who continue to send me encouraging notes through such social media as Facebook and Twitter.

On the pro football side, I want to thank the Tampa Bay Bucs organization, including owner Malcolm Glazer and general manager Mark Dominik.

My agents at IMG—Sandy Montag, Ben Stauber, and Max Teller—are opening doors that I could never open, let alone wheel through. It's exciting to partner with you, and we'll see what the future holds.

To my collaborator, Mike Yorkey, thanks for coming alongside me and helping me tell my story with great depth and emotion. Mike was backed up by Amy Bendell, a HarperCollins editor who pressed me to reveal more of my feelings.

Lisa Sharkey, the senior vice president and director of creative development at HarperCollins, was my champion throughout the publishing process. She believed in me and my story when many others didn't. Without Lisa, there would be no *Believe*.

A shout-out to Tim Tebow, who gave me a front-cover endorsement and gave us Broncos fans something to cheer about during a magical 2011 season. Tim, now that you're with the New York Jets, you just might make me a fan of the local team.

Finally, I want to thank my God—my Lord Jesus Christ—for giving me hope and eternal life. The Bible says that we will be given new bodies in heaven. Talk about something to look forward to!